CW00904565

SEARCHING FOR TENGA

BY MARIA BUCKINGHAM

ILLUSTRATED BY
CAROLIN SOUTHERN

£1 is donated to the Children's Hospital, Oxford,
a registered charity number 1057295

Order this book online at www.trafford.com/07-2650
or email orders@trafford.com

Most Trafford titles are also available at major online book retailers.

Note for Librarians: A cataloguing record for this book is available from Library and Archives Canada at www.collectionscanada.ca/amicus/index-e.html

Printed in Victoria, BC, Canada.

ISBN: 978-1-4251-5867-5

We at Trafford believe that it is the responsibility of us all, as both individuals and corporations, to make choices that are environmentally and socially sound. You, in turn, are supporting this responsible conduct each time you purchase a Trafford book, or make use of our publishing services. To find out how you are helping, please visit www.trafford.com/responsiblepublishing.html

Our mission is to efficiently provide the world's finest, most comprehensive book publishing service, enabling every author to experience success. To find out how to publish your book, your way, and have it available worldwide, visit us online at www.trafford.com/10510

www.trafford.com

North America & international
toll-free: 1 888 232 4444 (USA & Canada)
phone: 250 383 6864 ♦ fax: 250 383 6804
email: info@trafford.com

The United Kingdom & Europe
phone: +44 (0)1865 722 113 ♦ local rate: 0845 230 9601
facsimile: +44 (0)1865 722 868 ♦ email: info.uk@trafford.com

10 9 8 7 6 5 4 3 2

CONTENTS

To Georgia and Isaac
My 'Guinea-readers'

Chapter 1

Invasion!

Sam and Honey crept quietly along the passageway, hoping that no guards would notice that they had escaped from their prison cell. They were tiptoeing down the first flight of stairs when Honey suddenly stopped next to a window.

'Hey Sam!' he called, at the top of his voice. 'Just look at the view! I can see the whole city from here!'

'You absolute moron!' Sam ran back up the stairs, grabbed Honey by the tail and tried to drag him away. It was too late. Two burly guards came running towards them from around a corner, grabbed them and threw them back into their cell. The door slammed behind them with a sickening thud and they heard the disheartening sound of the key turning in the lock; the guards had secured the door again.

'Oh well,' said Honey, who talked with a slight lisp. 'At least we were able to stretch our legs, and that view was stunning, Sammy.'

'Shut up you idiot! I wish I had never had you as my brother, you just spoil everything.'

Sam flopped down on the pile of straw and scowled up at the confused Honey. Sam was a black dog, always tidy, with his raven black fur combed sleekly down. It seemed he gave up years ago trying to tidy the world. Instead, he put the same amount of effort into himself and his home, and left the world alone to its own folly of disorder!

In contrast, Honey, his older brother, who had a yellowish coat, was very untidy and always had his slightly longer fur all messy. He only combed it on *very* special occasions. Honey, likewise, seemed to have tried to better the world in his own way, by attempting to introduce it to the comfy joys of scruffiness. In this he succeeded to some extent, unlike his well-meaning brother. This was evident wherever he went and was now seen clearly in the state of his side of the small cell they shared. As well as his scruffiness, Honey's other obvious feature was his left eye, one half of which was bright red.

'Just think, Sammaramus, even if we had got as far as the gate they would have caught us and put us back in here.'

'You're a stupid dog, Honey,' answered Sam. Then, speaking more to himself, he continued, 'If only I had my sword, I would cut my way through every guard in the country and then…freedom, sweet freedom. The worse thing about a cell is there's no scope for adventure. If they had put us in a lake with crocodiles I wouldn't have minded so much, at least there would be drama, but this...!'

'A lake with crocs? Uh-uh, no way, not for me. Someone might get hurt!'

'You're supposed to be a soldier, Honey. You're supposed to be brave. If only there was a way out of here! Now we will rot here for the rest of our lives I suppose.'

'OK, Sammy, all we need is a huge earthquake and then we'll be out of here,' said Honey.

'Honey you know that we don't get earthquakes anymore. We just need courage, Honey; courage and brains!' Then, checking himself, he continued. 'I'm sorry I got cross with you. If we stick together we'll soon see it through.'

'That's right m'boy, that's right.'

'Now, let's think of a plan.' Sam walked to the tiny barred window and looked out. He could see, far down below, the prison courtyard. It had an irritating pattern on the floor, designed a long time ago by a dodgy tiger who claimed he was the best artist in Clawland. Rather than thinking of a new strategy for escape, Sam let his mind fly back again to the events that had brought him to this place.

His thoughts wandered back to a few weeks ago when he and Honey were living peacefully in the vast and beautiful city of Gilland. Bordered on one side by dense woodland, on the other it dipped its tail into the glassy sea. That city was the whole of the land of Gilland; and the land of Gilland the whole of the city. It stretched itself out over miles and miles of land, as if trying to reach the ends of the earth and grasp it to make itself even mightier. The buildings, houses and roads were a muddied white, as if they had been pure white at one stage, but the painting had got slightly damp and eroded, perhaps from the sea.

The streets smelled of many different things – spices, leather, fresh bread and meat. At every corner of the city centre there were civilians selling their goods that they had laboured so hard to produce. Behind these merchants a foreigner could speculate on the architecture of the houses and buildings, which had something of the Roman and something of Medieval.

The houses were of ridiculously different sizes, depending on the occupant of the house. If the occupant was an elephant, for example, it was just big all round. If it was a giraffe it was likely to be very tall; and a mouse's home would sometimes fall down when the bigger Gillandites caused an earthquake on their way to town. Because most of the inhabitants in Gilland were dogs, cats, tigers or bears, there was some housing size stability.

Sam longed for Gilland. It was *his* city and he loved it dearly. *Would we ever be able to go back there again?* he thought to himself.

The day it all started had just seemed like any normal day. The streets were crowded and young Gillandites played happily in the sunshine. King Faratol's Council was gathered together to decide for the ninth time whether it was undemocratic to have the Council comprised of mostly dogs. Because they were all dogs themselves, the majority vote was always predictable. The press didn't bother going to see the debate, but just stayed home and wrote about it there. There had been a murder the other day - a cat had eaten her next door neighbour, which happened to be a mouse. The Council had to get together on that important issue also and decided that, 'Yes it is disgraceful but we can't really do anything about it,' which was the same answer they gave when a giraffe went to visit a neighbour and accidentally made a hole in the roof.

However, that particular day, although appearing quite normal on the surface, had fearfully concealed a dark shadow. There had been rumours that the Clawlandites, a vicious and brutal nation, were going to invade. Faratol, the King, had not been his usual confident self and, as a result, his nation was restless and uneasy about the impending danger.

It happened so suddenly, thought Sam. *I was sitting down to a pleasant meal in the late evening with Honey when the woeful sound of the war trumpet sounded across the city and echoed back from the mountains, far away.*

He had assured his brother that the great army of the King would never let the invaders capture the city. But, deep inside, his confidence was failing and he knew that this war would be like none they had experienced before.

Sam jumped from the table and ran into his study. He opened the cabinet and removed the soft velvet cover to reveal his light-weight, gold sword that his father had given him. His father had fought many battles with this sword and died holding it in the defence of Gilland. He ran his paw along the blade and a sharp pain confirmed its keenness. He took down his armour. It was finely polished and sturdy. His helmet had the seal of his division in the army - a crown and the knight chess piece - on the forehead. He carefully attached his silk blue robe to show that he was a commanding officer of the Black Knights Division One. He quickly slid the sword into its sheath and ran out to the stable. He saddled his horse, Strawberry, and carefully put on its armour. He had mounted, and his horse had reared with anticipation. He was ready for battle.

At his post at the East gate he had called his five fellow knights together and they waited quietly for the attack. The silence was almost unbearable; the horses were restless and pawed the ground whilst the knights clutched their weapons tightly. Slowly and sullenly the smoke began to rise from the opposite side of the city. *They had taken them by surprise and attacked at the West gate and Gilland's fate was sealed,* Sam remembered.

The smoke grew and soon stretched over the city like a blanket of death. It obscured the moon and soon all he could see was the glow of the fire that ascended to the heavens and scorched all he had ever known. The smoke stung his nostrils. The smell was foul. Sam was powerless at that time to do anything. His heart throbbed; his eyes were streaming from the smoke - or was it from something else?

He shortened his reins and nudged his horse with his toes. The horse leaped into a gallop and flew up the highest hill in the city. Sam looked down on the destruction and saw the enemy army mercilessly killing his people. He clenched his fists in anger. The horse suddenly let out an eerie bray that echoed across the ruins of his city.

The next thing happened so quick, I was staring at the city when I felt a blow to my head and fell to the ground. I heard some voices and turned around to see some soldiers of the Clawlandites. I tried to get up and grab my sword, but the blow to my head had been heavy and I knew no more.

When he had come to, he found himself miles and miles away from Gilland, in the country of Clawland. He had been thrown into this revolting cell with his brother Honey, a soldier in the Rook Division One.

'We must get out and help free all the Gillandites taken captive.'

'What did you say, Sammy? You want to free all the other Gillandites? Why don't we just save our own skins and leave the others to get out themselves? It's way too dangerous to help other animals,' said Honey.

Sam laid his muzzle on the rough window ledge. 'They need our help, Honey, and we need them. A Gillandite should never leave another Gillandite to die, ever!'

Suddenly, they heard the sound of heavy feet walking along the corridor towards them. It got louder and louder and then stopped outside the door. Sam and Honey looked at each other with wide open eyes as they heard the sound of the rattling keys. The unknown being on the other side of the door unlocked it and it creaked slowly open. A huge lion, dressed all in black, entered. He held a scroll of paper.

'Lord Mould has issued your death warrants. You will be executed tomorrow morning.'

Chapter 2

No Time to Waste

'Right, we need to find a way out, Sammy! Quick, quick, quick!' Honey started flying around the cell, spraying straw everywhere.

'Calm down, Honey, there's no rush…'

'No rush? No rush? We're going to be executed *tomorrow*!'

'Just settle down, all we need is a good night's sleep and we'll have fresh minds to think in the morning.' Sam patted down his pile of straw, lay down and went straight to sleep.

Honey looked at his brother. *He's mad. He thinks I'm the one that doesn't know anything. All he can think of is how valiant he can look; he hasn't woken up to the real world yet.* There was a loud snore from Sam. *He's always content as long as there's something exciting going on, no matter how dangerous it is. He thinks he's brave, but I think he's just plain rash.*

Honey's thoughts dwelt on Sam for only a few seconds and then wandered back to their situation. *How are we going to get out of here?*

He suddenly had an idea. He slowly shoved Sam off the straw and gathered all the bedding together. He then started plaiting it and eventually he had the beginning of a very thin, precarious rope. The coarse rope cut into his paws as he worked, hour after hour, making it grow steadily longer and longer.

Sam woke up at the crack of dawn the next morning. He stretched and yawned as he tried to collect his thoughts together.

'Had a nice sleep last night, Honey-buns?' Honey just grunted in reply as he showed Sam the rope that had scraped the very skin off his paws.

'Honey! What in the world do you think you're going to use that for?'

'Sam, while you have been busy taking your beauty sleep, I have made us an ingenious way of escape. It took me hours and hours to think up this plan, but now I've got it. Throughout the ages to come, everyone will be able to look up to the *intelligent, quick-thinking* Honey and…'

'Alright Honey, just tell me what it is.' Sam had a half smile on his face; he was used to his brother and knew that the plan would be far from ingenious.

'Well, all we need to do is put this strong rope out the window.' Sam looked at the undoubtedly fragile rope and suppressed a smile as his brother continued. 'And then we climb out the window using this rope and then – simple – freedom.'

'Nice idea, Honey, but I don't think it will work quite as brilliantly as you think. Firstly, you may not have noticed those bars over the window. Secondly, that rope is just so pathetic; it couldn't even hold a fly!' Sam laughed now, ignorant of how his words had stung Honey, just as the ropes had stung him all night. If he had known, he would have been grateful for Honey's attempt.

Honey said nothing and quietly sat down and waited for Sam to tell him how to get out. He trusted Sam; he always had, even when they were little. He waited for Sam to take on the paternal role now.

'OK, let me see. We have approximately one hour to find a way out…' Sam walked around their tiny abode, looking at every single detail.

'What you doing, Sammy?'

'Well, when I was a squire, Dad showed me the whole plan of this prison. He worked here under disguise once and found out everything he could about it. He knew that there was a possibility of attack from the Clawlandites and knew that inside knowledge of this place would come in handy one day. He had great foresight, our Dad, and warned King Faratol long ago that the Clawlandites were the only army that we would never be able to defeat.'

Honey's mouth dropped open. 'Dad knew all that? Huh! Must have been really clever. I always knew I got it from somewhere.'

Then Sam said, more to himself than anybody, 'According to his plans, there should be a trap door somewhere in each cell.' He looked at the shadow created by the rising sun and looked frantically for the trap door. *It's not here!*

Just at that moment the door to the cell opened and a heavily armed guard appeared at the entrance. He grabbed Sam, while Honey cowered in a corner. Sam tried fighting off the guard and twisted around to ask Honey for help. But Honey was gone. Sam stopped struggling and stared in amazement. Soon another guard came.

'Where's the other one?' he asked.

'I don't know. He just disappeared,' said the first guard.

'Prisoners can't just disappear! Oh well, just take this one down to Lord Mould for his execution and we'll see what we can do about the yellow one later.'

They tied Sam's front paws together and led him down the steps. *This is the worst thing that could possibly happen! I'm completely powerless and Honey's on his own. He can't look after himself, he needs me.*

They led Sam down into a big hall filled to the four corners with Lord Mould's Clawlandites. They led Sam along the aisle to a place near to the front, where they tied him with strong ropes to an iron loop in the wall. Sam began to sweat as one of the Clawlandites prepared to usher in Lord Mould. Sam realised this was to be a trial and execution.

Just then a muffled voice was heard in the wall.

'Righto, let me see, Honey boy. Yes here we go; the passage leads this way. Ha, ha, if only Sam could see me now, he would have to admit that I *am* the cleverest dog in the world!'

Oh no, oh no! That's Honey speaking to himself. He

must have fallen through the trap door when he was huddled in that corner! Bother him! Why doesn't he keep quiet?

Honey's voice came out vividly from the wall, '"A good night's sleep" says Sam, "we'll have a clear mind in the morning" says Sam. He's mad that dog, absolutely mad. If he had spent the night searching for it instead of sleeping he would have found it. Now he's probably dead. Oh well, all good things must come to an end, except, of course, my intelligence, which will shine for ages to come.'

Sam thought quickly. He *had* to do something. He finally thought of the only one thing he could do – try and distract the Clawlandites' attention.

Sam suddenly started singing at the top of his voice. All the Clawlandites turned and stared at him.

'Gilland, Gilland, beautiful land,
When shall I see you again?
The crowded streets; the golden strand,
The land where joys shall never wane...'

And so he sung, getting redder and redder after every verse. He had to make the song up as he went along, as he hated singing and had never learned any songs. Sam had been convinced that songs would never be useful and therefore not worth the effort.

However, all his efforts were in vain. The Clawlandites began to get bored of Sam's 'talent' and turned their attention back to the talking wall.

'Hey, I think I can hear singing!' the wall said. And so the voice continued. And so the singing continued.

Finally, a Clawlandite of authority stood up to give encouragement to the others, who were becoming quite nervous.

'Right everyone, there is absolutely no cause to panic!' The effect of this was that everyone immediately started panicking and the hall was in chaos. The Clawlandites were a very superstitious lot, especially seeing as there were many superstitious ideas connected with their king – Lord Mould.

Amongst the crowd, Sam saw a soldier who had his golden sword! He ran up to Sam and threw it to him. Sam caught it and quickly cut himself free, wondering at this turn of fortune.

By this time the crowd was in a complete panic and nobody knew quite what was happening. Sam ran along the panelled wall, and tapped each panel in turn with the hilt of his sword. It merely made a light tap and he was beginning to give up hope. In frustration he threw his sword at one of the panels. The blade went right through and he heard a loud cry of pain from the other side.

He ran to the spot, picked up his sword again and quickly set to work, carefully removing the board. The removed panel revealed a gaping hole and he stepped through to find himself in a dark passageway. He quietly put the panel back into place as he heard the sound of the assembly trying to get organised again. Sam smiled, but the smile soon faded when he heard the voice of Lord Mould.

'Where is the culprit Gillandite? I have been looking forward to another execution!'

The voice sent an icy chill down Sam's spine; he shivered as he tried to picture what this evil lord must look like. But his thoughts turned quickly back to the tunnel he was in. It was pitch black and it smelt rank and musty, and when he leaned his paw against the side it felt wet and slimy.

'Honey!' he whispered.

From a few feet away he heard a groan. 'My goodness! My sword!'

He stumbled his way to where Honey was lying on the ground. His sword had cut Honey's left arm slightly. He ripped a sleeve off his prison clothes and wound it around the injured limb.

'I shall never see the light of day again, Sammaramus. Remember me when you're in your nice cosy cell, and I hope you will be able to survive without my intelligence.'

Sam told him to shut up and stop being such a coward. It wasn't a bad cut at all, just a little painful.

'At least it wasn't your right arm or you wouldn't be able to help me free the others.'

Honey suddenly sat up. 'Free the others! Sam…'

'Stop complaining. You have to face danger once in a while or else you'll never get through life.'

'But why should *we* free the others? We're not obliged to.'

'It's a Gillandite's duty to help other Gillandites, whatever the cost.' Sam helped Honey up and started running along the passage, back the way Honey had come.

'Are you mad, Sam? That's just where I've come from; it only leads back to the cells!'

'Exactly. We go to every cell and get the Gillandites out before Lord Mould kills them all. From what he said he must have murdered a lot of them already! I just hope he hasn't got to King Faratol yet.'

'Gillandite's duty indeed!' Honey grumbled as

Sam brushed some of the dirt off his clothes. Then together they groped along the dark passage that gaped greedily at them with its immense darkness looming in front of them.

Suddenly, Sam heard a rock tumbling along the floor. It stopped just behind them. Sam looked at it for a second and then stared into the darkness from whence they came. Somebody was there! And that somebody was following them.

'Who goes there? Stop! Tell me your name!' Sam shouted into the dismal darkness.

There was no reply.

'Look here, Sammy m'boy,' said Honey. 'I am under the strong impression that you are mad. There is nothing there. Besides, how do you know that that stone didn't just come here of its own accord? Ah, you didn't think of that now, did you? You see, if you had my intelligence...'

'Alright Honey, just be quiet now. You could be right; it may just be my imagination. At any rate, we can't just stand here while there's urgent work to be done.'

With that, Honey and Sam began walking along the passage again. But before long, Sam was sure that he could distinctly hear the sound of footsteps behind them. Honey must have noticed it too, for he didn't say anything but quickened his pace slightly. Sam quietly drew his sword and together they started running as fast as they could along the seemingly never-ending passage.

The footsteps also broke into a run behind them and got closer and closer. Soon, whatever it was that was following them was right behind them. Sam could hear its wheezy breath. He stopped abruptly in his tracks and wheeled around to face their mysterious follower.

Chapter 3

A Gillandite's Duty

'Tell me your name!' Sam clenched his paw around his sword. 'What's your business? Why are you following us?'

There was no reply.

'Give us a light, Honey,' said Sam. Honey took his tinder box and a candle out of his pocket, lit it and gave it to Sam. The ray of light shone on a very bedraggled fox. His fur was all ruffled so

Honey immediately took a liking to him. He wore the Gillandite armour so Honey concluded that all was safe and they had fortunately found a friend and not a foe. *Now perhaps we can get him to save all the other Gillandites while Sam and I just slip out to freedom,* Honey thought. His tail began to wag.

'What do you want?' Sam's voice was rough. Honey couldn't understand why he was still suspicious.

'I've come straight from King Faratol,' answered the fox. 'He has already escaped and is now making his way back to Gilland. If you follow me I'll take you to him.'

Sam scowled at the fox. 'Be off with you, you liar!' he said.

'Sam!' cried Honey. 'What do you think you're doing? Can't you see that this is a Gillandite, and now we don't have to free the others?'

'Leave all this to me, Honey. I know what I'm doing.' Then turning back to the fox, he said, 'Now listen here. You are to stay with me now, if you try and escape there will be severe consequences. Hand me that rope you made, Honey.'

Honey reached back into his pocket and produced the rope. He was very useful to Sam in that he always carried an unusual collection of useful things crammed into each of his pockets. Along with everything else, he always carried a pen and paper in his left pocket, just in case he had a moment of 'inspiration' for a poem. Sam never knew where he got these things, but some of them he made and some, I'm afraid to say, he stole from the guards when they weren't looking.

'I told you this rope would come in handy, Sam,' Honey was saying. Sam tied the fox's front paws together. It wasn't easy, as the rope was very flimsy. He finally succeeded and all three of them headed down the tunnel once more.

After they had walked for about half an hour the passageway began to slope sharply upward and led them into a huge room with dozens of doors lined along the walls. Sam asked Honey which one he had come out of, but Honey couldn't remember. In the end Sam just picked the one closest to them. He opened it and they stepped into a narrow tunnel which ended in another large room, just like the one they had left, with walls again lined with numerous numbers of doors.

'Dear me!' said Sam, 'this prison must have absolutely hundreds of cells!'

Once more they entered a door and it too led to a narrow tunnel, which in turn lead to another room full of doors. This carried on until they came to a room with eight trap doors in the ceiling.

'This is it,' Sam said. 'Each of these doors will lead to a separate cell.'

The ceiling was low enough for Sam to reach up and push one of the trap doors open. He jumped up, followed by Honey and the sulking fox.

When he got through the trap door, Sam found himself standing in a fairly big cell. To his immense joy, he saw King Faratol and the Queen. They were both noble-looking leopards and were very highly regarded in Gilland as just and peaceable monarchs.

'Your Highness,' Sam took a step back, clutched the hilt of his sword and bowed, in the usual Gillandite fashion. 'We have come to try and set the rest of Gilland free. Do you know of any way to let the others know about the trap doors so they can escape? Otherwise it would take an awful long time to go through all the trap doors to find them.'

'No problem,' said the King. He then went to one of the walls and gave a light tap. A muffled voice from the other side replied.

'Pass on the message that there is a trap door in each cell,' the King said. 'Send the message on that everyone must go through the trap door and we'll all meet somewhere at the bottom.' Then he turned towards Sam. 'Right, we had better follow you out to meet the others. The message will get around pretty quick, there's no soundproofing between each cell.'

It wasn't long before all the remaining Gillandites were assembled in the first great room that Sam, Honey and the fox had entered. Sam had watched carefully to see which door it was that no Gillandite came from. It was the second to the end on the right.

'Right everyone, follow me,' cried Sam, 'this door here must be the one that leads out of the prison.'

Sam entered the door and all the others followed. It sloped sharply down for a few minutes before straightening out. They seemed to walk along it for ages until Sam heard the sound of water above the tunnel. *That must be the river,* he thought. Eventually the tunnel sloped sharply up and they soon found themselves just inside the dense forest that covered half of the world.

The Gillandites walked as quietly as they could, deeper and deeper into the dark forest, until they were far enough from any chance of being detected. But still King Farratol urged them to walk on; on until the sun began to rise; on until the sun was high in the sky; on until the sun was sinking behind the trees. They finally came to a stop in a vast clearing.

'We'll camp here,' King Faratol said. So all the Gillandites set up their tents from the blankets and leather they had managed to barter from peaceful traders on the way.

Honey was sitting under a tree all on his own, so Sam came to sit next to him to cheer him up. Sam had noticed that Honey had been gloomy and silent all the way from the prison.

'What's the matter with you, Honey-buns?' asked Sam.

Honey didn't reply, but instead turned away and faced his back toward Sam.

'You're cross with me, Honey, aren't you? What is it about?'

Honey turned towards Sam again.

'Well, it's not fair. Everyone thinks you're the gallant one, that you're the hero, and they just ignore me. It was me who found the passageway after all! It was me who supplied you with my ingenious rope and the candle! It's not fair! It's just not fair!'

Sam smiled and suppressed a laugh.

'Of course, Honey, of course. We all know that you played probably the biggest part in it, but the thing is they never appreciate those that play the important roles. They just like to choose the one they'd rather look up to as hero. Besides, I know I couldn't have managed anything, especially the stay in the cell, without your sense of humour!'

Honey didn't know whether to take this as a compliment or not, but decided in the end that he liked Sam anyway and didn't really want to be cross with him. So he condescended to talk to the one who stole his praise.

'Sammy, how did you know that the fox was really from Mr Mould's army and was trying to trick us?'

'Oh, simple. I noticed that he didn't have the seal of the king on his helmet, so I knew that the armour was forged.'

And so they talked pleasantly on, late into the night beside a roaring fire.

Early the next morning, Sam was woken up by one of the King's servants.

'King Farratol needs to speak to you urgently.'

Sam got up and walked over to the King's tent. The King was inside playing chess with the Clawlandite fox.

'Ah, Sam, I need to talk to you,' said the King. Sam sat down to hear what Farratol had to say. 'I wondered if you would like to accompany me to visit the Great Eagle?'

Sam's mouth dropped open. 'The Great Eagle?'

'Yes. The Great Eagle is the most powerful animal in the world. Lord Mould is the second most powerful...thing, in the whole world. So it follows that the Great Eagle will be the only one able to protect us from the ever tightening iron grasp of Lord Mould.'

'Oh, but I thought that we were safe from Lord Mould now?'

'No. As I was going to say, we Gillandites are the third most powerful nation and one of those that Lord Mould needs to defeat in order to rule all the four corners of the earth. After he has defeated Gilland of the West, he will go on to capture the Endworld of the South; then finally he will wage war with the Great Eagle who rules the North. Once he has power over the four corners of the earth, he will have power over the whole world itself. He's a tyrant and a greedy ruler, so we must fight against him to save Gilland and in turn save the world.'

'I see,' said Sam.

'But the Great Eagle is proud and self-willed, and will not protect any nation unless they make an agreement with him. He doesn't live far from here, just up on that mountain over there...' The King pointed to a tall mountain that reached up to the sky and disappeared above the clouds. 'I sent a messenger to ask whether I could come and visit for the purpose of an agreement. He sent the message back saying he would be delighted. So...'

'You want me to come with you,' Sam finished his sentence.

'In short, yes.'

Sam bowed and then stepped outside the tent. He bumped right into Honey who had been outside, listening in to the conversation.

'I can come too, can't I Sam? I can can't I?'

'No Honey, not this time. I'm sorry.'

'Can't you just say you're busy, Sammy, and then we can go and explore this forest together?'

'No Honey, it's my duty as a Gillandite to protect the King. That's why we had to free him from the prison, and that's why I have to go with him now. I know nothing about this mysterious Great Eagle but I have a feeling that he's a dangerous sort. That's why I have to go and make sure that the King is kept safe whilst he has this conference with the eagle.'

Honey's head drooped and his tail tucked under as he walked slowly back to his tent.

'I'm sorry Honey,' Sam shouted after him, 'I really am sorry.' He then went to his own tent to put on his armour and saddle Strawberry. Once he was ready, he mounted his horse and rode back to the King's tent. The King leopard was already mounted on his thoroughbred that was given to him as a gift by the kind Hooflandites.

'Ready Sam?' King Faratol asked.

'Yes, your Highness.'

'Then let's go!' He kicked his horse and they were soon galloping up the steep mountain to a very forbidding-looking castle. The castle was all grey and stained from the wet clouds, and looked over its fluffy enemy with a disapproving eye.

Sam and the King rode up to the 'eye'. It was a huge door with a large gold engraving on it. The engraving was of an eagle leading an army against another army, which was led by...by...Sam couldn't see the one leading the enemy army, for it had been too badly eroded by the clouds.

'That engraving was put there by the Great Eagle. It's a battle that was fought a long time ago by him when he was just gaining his power,' explained King Farratol. 'A battle against Lord Mould, and he won. It's a pity that this engraving is eroded. I've never seen Lord Mould - did you see him when you were about to be tried in Clawland?'

'No, I didn't actually.'

'Oh well, probably better that you hadn't, for other animals say that he looks indescribably frightening, and then they never could actually describe what he looked like in detail because it was too awful.'

'Is Lord Mould an animal?'

'Oh no, not an animal; he despises animals. He's just simply a...a...a thing.'

Just then the door groaned and screeched as it slowly opened.

Chapter 4

The Great Eagle

As the door swung open, Sam was gripped with a strong feeling of apprehension. If the outside of the castle was so mysterious and grand, what would it be like on the inside? What would this Great Eagle be like?

The door keeper was a large rabbit. It fixed its eyes on Sam and the King as if trying to communicate something but not daring to speak it out loud. The mysterious door keeper was dressed in a strange type of garment; intricately embroidered with tiny figures – animals, trees, but most prominent was the golden embroidery of an Eagle with its talons stretched out ready to grasp at a small puppy.

Sam turned his wondering attention away from the garment and to the face of the rabbit, who then began to speak in a strained whisper.

'Are you the King that's come to make the... agreement with his worship?' Sam looked sharply at the animal.

'I am, as you say, King Farratol, and I demand to see the Great Eagle,' said the King.

The rabbit drew in a deep breath and looked terrified when King Farratol said 'demand'. Nevertheless, he consented to the demand and turned to lead them to the throne room. Sam took special notice of his surroundings as he was keen to remember it all to tell Honey when he got back to camp.

They were led along a long corridor, dimly lit with candles. The candles did not flicker or waver, but kept completely still, as if they, too, like the door keeper, were afraid to move a muscle wrongly. The frightened candles cast their rays onto the walls of the corridor, revealing huge paintings and tapestries. Each and every tapestry and painting had the Great Eagle in it – from detailed studies of battles that the Eagle had won, to portraits of the same at banquets and balls.

Sam stopped at one tapestry and stood staring at it. It was the same embroidery as the one on the rabbit's garment. Sam looked closer at the face of the little puppy. The needlework was so detailed that he could observe the pained and frightened expression on its face. He could see it so vividly that his heart throbbed and melted with sympathy for the young creature.

He was suddenly drawn away from the picture by the realisation that the King was far ahead of him, still being led along the endless hallway. He caught up, but his mind was preoccupied by that strange tapestry. He knitted his brows and thought to himself, *Why does this simple picture attract my attention so much? Is it because it's a puppy and that's why it tugs on my heartstrings? Or is there something else? And why does the Great Eagle appear to be about to kill this pup? Surely it's just a harmless puppy?* However hard he tried, he could not shake the image from his mind.

Finally, their guide stopped in front of a massive door – everything seemed to be enormous and grand in this strange place! The door opened in response to a light tap from the rabbit. Then they stepped inside a vast hall with a large solid ruby throne at the opposite end. On the throne was a magnificent golden eagle.

Sam and Farratol stopped and stood in awe. Then, prompted by the rabbit, they walked to the foot of the throne and bowed. The Eagle set its keen eye on the visitors.

'Ah, here you are at last!' he said, in a voice that seemed so normal in contrast to his physical grandeur. 'You've come for the agreement, have you? Very well. But I warn you, that you're sure to fail with your side of it.' With this encouragement, the Great Eagle descended from his throne and invited them to sit down with him at a beautiful mahogany table.

The King and the Great Eagle talked for over two hours, trying to come to a unanimous decision on the terms of the agreement.

'This is my last offer to you,' said the Great Eagle, finally. 'Farratol, King of Gilland, I will give you a leopard cub that I have nurtured as if he were my own son.' Here he looked at Sam, and then back to the King. 'You then shall take him to your home and bring him up yourself, for I, the Great Glorious Eagle, cannot spare the time from my pleasure-seeking to tutor him myself. That is my last offer. Take it or leave it. You realise yourself, Farratol, King of Gilland, that Lord Mould and the Clawlandites are even now preparing to attack. They will not destroy the nation of Gilland if they know I'm protecting you. No one can defeat me! Every nation quakes before me! If you do choose to accept my offer, you will be safe from threat, but if ever the leopard cub is lost you will be protected no longer! Now, do you accept my offer or not?'

Sam looked at the perplexed face of the King.

'I accept the offer.'

The Eagle flapped its wings with pleasure and pride.

'Now you may go from my presence. My servants shall show you your apartments, and tomorrow morning I will introduce you to the cub.'

Two rabbits came, wearing garments just like the first, except each had different embroideries on them. They lead them up a flight of winding steps into a large sitting room with two doors leading into two luxurious bedrooms.

'These are your sleeping quarters. I hope they are comfortable enough for you to be able to think clearly on what you have just gone and got yourselves into!' said one of the servants. Then both of the rabbits disappeared through the door and back down the flight of stairs. Sam got up to close the door behind them, and then sat down opposite the King.

'This *is* a strange, strange place!' said Farratol. 'Do you think I did right in accepting the offer?'

'I suppose that's all you could do really,' answered Sam.

'Still, I wonder why he gave us such an easy task to complete our side of the treaty – looking after a leopard cub! Oh well, at least it's a leopard, the same as myself; it will make it easier for my wife. It sounds suspicious to me; perhaps the Great Eagle is trying to trick us.'

'Could be.'

'You're not very talkative, what's the matter?'

'Nothing. I'm just thinking about a picture I saw, that's all.'

The King shrugged his shoulders. 'A picture eh? Oh well, I think we ought to go to bed and get some sleep. I expect tomorrow will be quite an interesting day. Perhaps it's because the cub is very rowdy and hard to manage.'

It felt like only a few minutes to Sam before the sun rose the next morning. His dreams had been very troubled. The two Gillandites made their way to the throne room, very keen to find out what this mysterious cub was like. The Great Eagle was standing near the entrance, ready to receive them.

'I've just ordered one of my servants to get the cub, so he should be here very soon.'

The Great Eagle strutted around the room, waiting for the strangers to ask him questions about his glory and riches. Sam quickly realised that something was expected of them and asked about the engraving on the door.

'Ah ha, yes, the engraving!' he seemed very pleased about being asked this, and told them all about his victory in that battle. He then went on to explain some of the tapestry and paintings in the hallway. Sam waited and hoped that he'd explain the one picture he was interested in, but the Eagle finished speaking and waited for more questions.

Sam plucked up courage and asked. 'There's one of your pictures I particularly like.'

'Of course, of course,' the Eagle chuckled to think that he had made such an impression on his visitors.

'The picture I'm interested in is the one of you about to snatch up that little pup…'

The Great Eagle beat his wings together in rage and fixed a fiery eye on the inquirer.

'Do not ask me about that picture, Sam, Knight of Gilland, son of Rocky!' he thundered. *If he finds out,* thought the enraged bird, *about that picture…*

Just then, the leopard cub was brought in and the noble Eagle soon calmed down.

'This is the cub,' he said.

The King looked at the cub. It was very quiet, and when he looked straight into its eyes he saw a kind, sad expression that seemed to have a longing to be loved and to love. Farratol's and Sam's hearts softened to the young creature immediately.

'Well, this is he,' said the Eagle. 'I hope you will give him a good education. He has been no trouble to me, but has been quite content to find companionship in his books and keep himself out of mischief.'

And indeed, his only companions were his books. When he was taken up to Sam and the King's apartment, he was soon sitting on the window-sill reading a fairy tale book. He sat there late into the evening, while Sam and the King busied themselves with other matters.

After a while, the King went to bed and Sam approached the little reader.

'Are you going to bed? Or are you too absorbed in that book? Is it interesting?'

The lonely youngster looked into Sam's smiling face. He read Sam's face and found pity and friendliness.

'What's your name little cub?'

'Tenga.'

'That's a nice name. Mine is Sam. Not really very interesting is it?'

'Names don't matter.'

'I suppose you are right.'

Tenga grew confident. 'I like reading fairy tales because they always have a good ending. Do you think I will ever live happily ever after, Sam?'

Sam's heart melted. 'I'm sure you will. When we get back to the Gillandite camp I'll introduce you to Honey, my brother. There are also lots of other young animals for you to play with.'

'Play? I'd like to try and do that! In my book there was a little human boy who played with other boys, and I always wanted to learn how to do it.'

They talked late into the night, as Tenga introduced Sam to all his 'book friends'; each of the characters in the books were friends to this friendless cub. Sam felt he had learned a lot that night as he pondered over the strange events and his new young friend. But there were so many unanswered questions in his mind, especially about that picture.

Why can't I keep my mind off it! What IS it about that puppy? Why was the Great Eagle so cross about my asking about it? Is there something he doesn't want me to know?

How did he know my name, job and father? What about Tenga? Why was the Great Eagle so keen to have us look after him? Why does he always have rabbits as servants? Why are the servants so afraid all the time? Why…? Why…? Why…? And so the 'Whys' haunted him the whole night through; he was so deep in thought that he hardly heard the patter of rain on the roof and the distant roll of thunder.

Chapter 5

An Important Discovery

The weather was in that undecided state, when it is sunny one moment and slightly clouded the next. Sam, King Faratol and little Tenga set off for the Gillandite camp.

'I tell you what,' said Sam to no one in particular and to the world in general, 'I'm sure glad to be out of that place. That Eagle is so peculiar!'

Getting no reply from the world in general, Sam

subsided into silence again. They pushed their horses into a trot and Sam was quite disgusted to see that Tenga could not ride his pony very well at all. *What on earth did the Eagle teach the cub if he didn't teach him riding! Riding is number one priority!* But soon Sam was freed from his thoughts when they reached the camp.

'There, Tenga, there's your home for the meantime!' cried Sam. He then started cantering down the hill towards the camp, keen to see Honey again.

Tenga looked down on the many tents stretched out before him, snuggled among the fir trees. It was a welcome site, so modest!

They were greeted by a crowd of animals, all curious to find out what the agreement was. But Honey was the happiest of all to see them home. As soon as Sam dismounted, Honey ran straight towards him, but in his haste he couldn't stop and crashed straight into him. Once this enthusiastic greeting was over, Sam introduced Honey to his young friend. Tenga looked dubiously at the boisterous Honey but liked him immediately, and Honey took him away to meet the other young animals.

'You needn't mind Sam, Tenga, he's just a little mad. If only he had the brains that I have.' Here

Honey let out a long sigh. 'You see, without me, Sammy would be in all sorts of trouble. It's a miracle he survived without me when he visited that Eagle guy.'

And so Honey talked on and on while Tenga kept silent, his sad eyes looking up with curiosity every now and then. He seemed to read something in Honey's face. Surely he had seen that face somewhere before? He had felt sorry for that face, he had found a companion in that face before, but where?

Soon he forgot about Honey and stopped to watch some young animals playing. Playing? Ah, what a phenomenon to see real life playing! He paid special attention to a young owl that seemed very knowledgeable in the game of tag they were playing, and after the game he introduced himself to him.

'Tenga? What an interesting name! My name is Owl. You see, my parents had ten other little owls and had run out of original names by the time they came to me.'

'You have brothers and sisters?'

'Sure I do, but they're such a bother. I'm the youngest so they think they can boss me around, but I'll teach them one of these days! Besides, I'm the best flyer of all my family!'

Tenga enjoyed his new friend's light careless chatter; he enjoyed his light manner and friendliness. *Just like that human boy in my book! It's like a dream; all my book friends are coming to life!*

Owl stopped talking for a minute and looked Tenga all over. He seemed undecided and then came to a conclusion.

'I like you! Come, let's go and play.'

For probably the first time in his life, Tenga's face lit up with a smile.

'What games do you know? I bet the Great Eagle had some fun ones up his sleeve!'

Tenga remarked that he didn't think the Great Eagle had a sleeve, and he didn't play games anyway.

'What in the world did you do all day?'

'I read books, lots of books. I even read human books.'

'Wow! Human books? Did ya bring any with you?'

'Yes, a few.'

'Right! You gotta let me see them!'

They spent that whole afternoon together. Tenga read his worn-out books to the spell-bound owl, until Sam called them into the dining room for supper. The table was only just big enough for Sam, the two friends and Honey.

'Hey, Sammaramus, you have to tell me about your visit now. Did you have fun?' asked Honey at the end of the meal.

'First of all, Honey-buns and all present, I need to tell you about more immediate matters.' Sam pushed his chair back from the table. 'I was just talking to the King, and he said that Lord Mould has, for some strange reason, given us back Gilland. We are to pack our belongings and move back there tomorrow morning.'

There was a murmur of approval.

'Now, as for this Great Eagle,' Sam continued. 'It was a very strange place, that's all there is to it really. I saw one thing that really attracted my attention, though, and I haven't been able to get it out of my mind.'

'Out with it then Sammy, what was it?'

'Oh, just an old tapestry of the Great Eagle swooping down on a little yellow…' Sam's voice trailed off. His face took on a sickly colour as he stared at Honey's face. Honey was rather alarmed at this, wondering whether Sam was so shocked at him for forgetting to wash his face that morning.

'What's the matter, Sam? What was the yellow thing? Carry on with the story and ignore my face, I'll wash it after dinner.'

'Honey…' Sam gulped. 'Nothing, it was

nothing.'

'So you saw a yellow nothing? Well! I think you had better go straight to bed. I knew that you would lose what mind you had if I didn't go with you. I did warn you.' Honey shook his head very slowly. 'Just go to bed, you'll feel a lot better tomorrow.'

He patted Sam gently on the head. Sam exchanged glances with Tenga. *I knew I had seen his face before!* thought Tenga. *What can this all mean?*

Chapter 6

Unnatural Things

It was so good to be back in beautiful Gilland! They had had a lot of work on their hands to restore it to its former glory, but now it looked as pure as ever. Tenga was delighted with his new home and city, and Sam had taken him and Owl on as squires to eventually qualify as black knights of Gilland.

Tenga enjoyed his training and Sam equally

enjoyed teaching him. Tenga was a very promising rider and Sam took delight in his steady and sure progress. But Owl was not so quick to learn. He had fallen off countless times, mainly because it was hard to hold on with wings, but partly because he didn't have as much enthusiasm for it as Tenga.

Every afternoon, when the training had finished for the day, Tenga and Owl went to Honey's house to play. It was the house that Sam and Honey had grown up in and Sam watched them with delight as they played, just as he had played with Honey all those years ago. Tenga and Owl would often sit down in the evening and Tenga would read to Owl out of the books that had been such friends to him in the lonely castle of the Great Eagle, just as Sam had read to Honey. Tenga and Owl played in the old gnarled tree outside and pretended to be great Gillandite knights, fighting dragons and winning battles; just like Honey and Sam had done. They ran around the house and filled the long silent rooms with laughter. Sam observed all of this and at such times his eyes would twinkle and his tail wag.

In such a manner time flew pleasantly by and the young squires were nearly ready to be knighted. Sam decided to take them riding in the forest and hunt for one last time before he was satisfied that they were ready.

They rode into the forest and chased a number of deer, but the windy weather made the quarry alert and fast, so they didn't catch anything. Eventually they gave up and stopped for a break. Owl was summoned by his mother because he had a flying lesson that could not be missed, so Tenga and Sam were left on their own to talk and sit under the shade of a large oak tree. The tree was on a kind of large ledge that overlooked the noble city of Gilland. Behind them the forest stretched itself to the mountain range of the north. On the highest mountain they could just glimpse a shining speck which was the Great Eagle's castle.

Tenga rolled over onto his belly and bit contentedly at the long grass. There was the scent of spring in the air and the birds sang to each other in the treetops above. They sat for a long time, with Tenga quietly musing as he often did, and Sam beginning to get restless as he often did. Soon Sam got fed up with doing nothing and tried to engage the quiet Tenga in conversation.

'You seem to be happier here than you were with the Great Eagle, Tenga?'

'I am, especially with a friend like Owl.'

'Do you think you are ready to be a real knight of Gilland?'

'There's nothing that I would like better than to fight for my new country.'

Sam smiled. Tenga's words were almost the same as his the day before his father knighted him.

'I know I've only been here for a few months but I love this nation and wouldn't leave it for the world. I've been so looking forward to being knighted.'

'And you will be an honourable knight!'

Just then, Sam saw Owl flying towards them. *As for him, I think I might have to work on his riding a bit longer. Tenga possesses a skill that I've seen in none of my previous squires.* Sam was a proud knight and looked forward to knighting the prince of Gilland as much as Tenga did. *Tomorrow will be a day to remember!*

Owl landed next to Tenga and asked him in his cheerful way whether he would like him to demonstrate what he had just learned in his flying lesson. Tenga readily agreed and Sam watched the young animals with pleasure as Owl and Tenga ran off to play.

Owl demonstrated his reckless flying skills.

'Now,' said Owl, as he alighted back on firm ground, 'I'm going to teach you how to fly!' He was joking of course, and Tenga laughed, but he agreed that it would be fun to play at it.

'Come up this tree. This is how Mum taught me.

Right now, just jump down and flap your paws together. I'll be here at the bottom to catch you, then you can go on my back and we can pretend you're flying! Come, try it!' Owl flapped around the tree in excitement as Tenga jumped down. He got ready to swoop underneath Tenga to catch him, but then…

'Tenga! Tenga! You're actually flying!' screamed Owl, as Tenga mysteriously began to rise instead of fall! 'You're high enough now Tenga, come back towards me. Tenga?' But something was wrong. Tenga was not in control of what he was doing, and was calling piteously to Sam for help. Sam rose quickly and ran to the foot of the oak.

'Owl, fly up there quick and grab Tenga.' *Oh dear, what is this all about!*

But it was all too late, for Tenga had disappeared into a cloud that had just formed. The sky was now overcast and a thunderbolt of lightning struck quite near to the bewildered owl and dog, the crack of it half deafening Sam for a few seconds. The rain came down in sheets, and it was very dark.

Sam shouted over the noise of the rain and thunder for Owl to go home as quickly as he could, then he called and called Tenga's name. There was no reply. *No, no, not Tenga! Anyone but*

Tenga! Oh come back Tenga, come back!

He waited for over an hour, getting drenched to the skin, then began to realise that the innocent little cub was lost. He rode down the slippery slope into Gilland and cantered to Honey's house.

'Oh Honey, what shall we do now? Tenga is lost; the nation is lost; all is over.' Sam was soon wrapped around with a blanket, and Honey was lighting the candles as the dark storm continued to rage outside.

'I wouldn't worry, Sam,' said Honey. 'With my brains we can find him immediately. You are forgetting what a genius I am, you silly old doggy!'

Sam relaxed his tight grip on the arm of his chair as he found comfort in his brother.

'I can always rely on you, Huns, to cheer me up. But so many unnatural things are happening! A weird Great Eagle; a piece of artwork that makes an impression on me!'

'I must admit, Sammaramus m'boy, you never really were the sort of person to appreciate art. I myself am a great artist; you remember that picture of a house I once drew?'

Sam ignored Honey's question, even though he remembered the picture, though at the time he had to ask him what it was.

'And now this! A leopard that disappears into

the clouds, and a storm that starts up at the very same second! Poor little Tenga. One day, Honey, we will wake up and find that this is all a bad dream.'

'Who said we were in a bad dream? Sam, just admit it, you're a little bit confused, aren't you? Now, if you had my brains you would be able to work these things out clearly. For example, you don't know why Tenga disappeared through the clouds. Well, I'll tell you: it must have been because he went through the clouds and then the clouds were between you and him. That's why he *disappeared* through the clouds. Really, Sammy, I *am* surprised at your stupidity.' Honey shook his head slowly again, which he had a habit of doing when he talked about Sam's low intelligence. 'You have great reason to be happy, my unhappy brother, because I have composed another one of my fantastic songs. It took me ages to write it, but just you listen.'

Honey pulled out a piece of paper from a drawer, cleared his throat and began to sing at the top of his voice.

'My name is Honey,
Not as in that food that is sticky and runny,
My name isn't really funny,

Because it was given to me by my Mummy.'

He paused for breath and to ask Sam, 'Do you like it?'

Sam, who was at this stage beginning to laugh, said that he liked it very much, and asked the pleased Honey to continue.

'My brother's called Sam and he's mad
Which is really very sad
But he's not bad,
Just mad.'

And so he sung on, the verses getting more and more ridiculous. When he had finally finished, the storm had stopped and it was already night. Sam was in a happier mood when he went to bed and tried not to think on the disaster that had just occurred.

Early next morning Sam put on his best clothes and walked to the palace to talk to the King. Everything seemed so quiet and empty now that he had lost his promising young squire.

'Where's Tenga, Sam?' the King asked. 'The Queen's been sick with worry over where he's got to. He didn't come back last night after the riding lesson. I hope he didn't get caught in that awful storm last night.'

Sam eyed the chess game. Of late the King had been spending an extraordinary amount of time playing chess with the Clawlandite fox that Honey and he had found in the tunnel of the prison. Again, the fox was winning. He drew his thoughts away from the King's strange behaviour to the situation in hand.

'Tenga is missing.'

The King turned pale and absentmindedly put a glass pawn chess piece into his mouth. He soon realised it was there and spat it out. But as Sam described the way in which Tenga had gone missing, Faratol absentmindedly put another glass chess piece in his mouth. This time it was a knight and he almost choked.

Then the King thought hard for a while, and finally spoke up.

'Sam, if Tenga went up above the clouds, he must have found a way up there. Perhaps there's a rope or something. Go back to that oak and climb up and I'm sure – I know – you will find a way to where Tenga is now.'

So Sam went outside, mounted his horse and rode to the oak tree. But just as he trotted up to it he noticed a ring of fire around it. Within a matter of seconds, the fire leapt up and the whole tree was in flames. *Who set that tree alight?* thought Sam. *This is very odd. Tenga must have been kidnapped, and that kidnapper doesn't want us to know where Tenga is!*

He looked around to see if he could find the culprit. He espied a dark shadowy creature disappearing quickly behind the trees. Sam spurred his horse into a gallop to pursue the strange figure. The hoof beats of his steed pounded heavily against the ground as if the heart of the whole world was racing with excitement.

He galloped around the forest chasing the creature; but it seemed to disappear behind the trees and then reappear somewhere else, as if it was teasing Sam. But eventually the creature lost interest in the chase and disappeared completely.

I've lost him! thought Sam, as he turned his horse back to Gilland. *What will happen to us now? Lord Mould will wage war and we shall lose without the protection of the Great Eagle.*

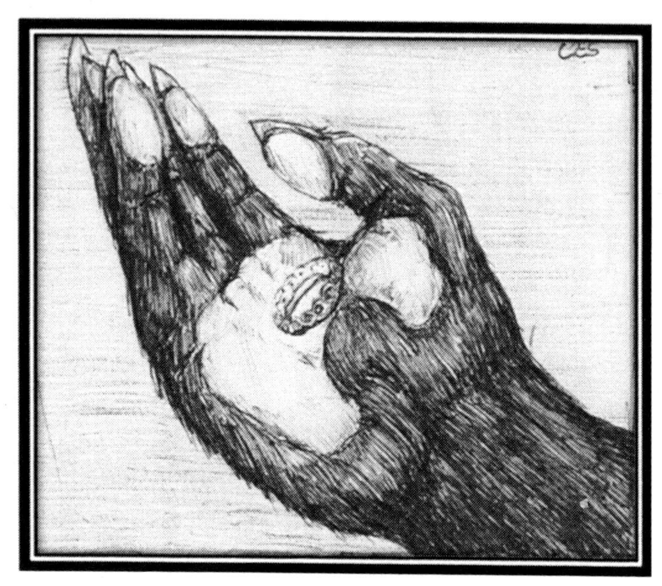

Chapter 7

The Commission

Sam rode slowly down into Gilland and along the busy main street. *What was that mysterious creature? Why did it not want me to get to the tree?* thought Sam to himself as he rode towards Honey's house.

Honey had promised him a special meal when he came back, and Sam was looking forward to spending a carefree evening with his brother. But just then, he pulled his horse to a stop as he saw two of the King's messengers, a bear and a weasel, hurrying towards him. He drew his sword and touched the messengers' swords with it, in the usual fashion of greeting between soldiers.

'The King requires your presence.' The bear messenger sheathed his sword and waited for Sam's reply.

'I'm so sorry but I have an appointment with my brother, he's made a meal all by himself and…'

The messenger raised his eyebrows.

'…I just can't disappoint him,' Sam continued. 'He would be so upset that I wouldn't hear the last of it.'

The weasel reached into his pocket and brought out a golden ring lined with rubies. He placed it in Sam's paw.

'A commission ring? What on earth does the king want with me?' Sam turned the commission ring around and around. A commission ring was a very rare and important gift from the king of a country. It meant that the king wished the recipient to complete a serious errand or mission. The bearer of a commission ring was given an authority recognised throughout the world to do any reasonable act to have the commission fulfilled.

'Better go and find out what the commission is,'

muttered Sam to himself. 'Honey will have to wait.'

He followed the messengers to the palace and into the throne room. The King was playing chess with the Clawlandite fox again! Why? Has his old obsession come back? Sam could see clearly that the King was losing the game again.

King Farratol paused the game and turned towards Sam.

'You got the commission, Sam?' asked the King. 'Good.' He sat down on his throne and had a bit of trouble trying to sort his robes out. He called to his servants to bring his crown.

This must be something very important, thought Sam, *if he needs to put on his crown before telling me what the commission is.*

After the King finally managed to get the crown, which was slightly too big, to sit steady on his head and not slip over his eyes, he continued.

'This fox is a spy,' he pointed to the Clawlandite fox that was standing at the King's left hand side. 'He has been spying on Lord Mould for a while, reporting back on his position regarding Gilland…Oh bother!' The crown had fallen over his eyes again and this time had struck him painfully on his muzzle. He rubbed the sore spot as he talked on.

'This fox has recently just come back from Clawland and has found out that Lord Mould is preparing for battle. The furnaces are burning red hot all day as the Clawlandites make weaponry and armoury. It seems that they gave us back Gilland to make us unaware of his evil intentions towards us. He means to kill us all; to wipe out the whole of Gilland in one tremendous shock.'

'Then we will fight them!' cried Sam, drawing out his sword with a gleam of excitement in his eyes.

'Yes, we will fight them…' again the crown slipped over the King's eyes. He took it off and threw it forcefully across the room. 'But we will lose!' he shouted.

Sam slid his sword back into its sheath. 'What will you have me to do? I can fight until I drop dead. My horse and my sword, not to mention the blood of my noble father in my veins, have never failed me yet.'

'I don't want your skill in battle, neither your sword nor Strawberry to fight this battle, not yet. I want all those for a different, more important, task. Your commission that you hold in your paw is to find Tenga. The only slight possibility of winning this battle is if the Great Eagle and his army help us. Tenga is the key to that. You *must* find him!'

'How? Where?'

'Anywhere! Wherever you think best; just keep on looking until you find Tenga. Sam, it's our only hope.'

Sam dropped the ring into his pocket – a sign that he will take on the task.

'Good.' The King slapped his paws on his knees in satisfaction. 'You must go tomorrow morning. Take whom you will. That is all.'

Sam took a step back, clutched the hilt of his sword and bowed, then hurried out of the palace and got to Honey's house, just in time to see a thin column of smoke issuing from the kitchen window. Honey rushed out, shouting that the food was burned and spoilt.

'I'm so sorry Honey, but I had an important meeting with the King.' Sam and Honey walked inside and tried to salvage as much of the dinner as possible. Sam had no idea what the meal was supposed to be - it looked like the slop given to pigs, he thought. It tasted like it too. He was very brave, however, and managed to eat all the 'food' on his plate.

After the meal, Sam browsed through Honey's collection of books. Honey was a keen collector and collected almost anything, his collection of rare and old books being his most useful. Sam took out a book called *History, Geography and General Observations of Strange Plants and Creatures.*

'This might help,' said Sam, as he took the dusty old book out of the bookcase. It was large and heavy, so he put it on the table to read. He opened it at the page describing the creature called the Gronad.

'The Gronad, that's it! Of course, the Gronad must have captured Tenga. It all makes sense!' Sam banged the table with his paw, bringing Honey running from the kitchen, where he was washing up, to see what all the excitement was about.

'Alright, Honey-buns, do you feel like travelling, adventure and excitement?'

'Sounds fun. Tell me all about it Sammy.'

Sam explained all about the commission and talked about the likely places to look and speculated about all the adventure that they could run into.

'Sounds really good Sam. Of course you'll need my brains, you're not clever enough to do this alone. One question, though: does this mission commission thingy involve any kind of danger of any kind? And do you expect me to do any fighting? You know my brains are far too valuable to get hurt in any way, I have to look after them.'

'In short, Honey, it probably will involve a lot of

danger and all that. But don't worry about looking after your brains. We would suffer no loss if they were disposed of.'

'What does 'disposed of' mean, Sam?'

'Never mind,' said Sam with a half smile on his face.

'Hang on a sec. Did you say there would be danger?'

'I believe I did.'

'Right. OK. I'm out. Can't go. Far too busy. Have a nice time with it Sam!'

'Honey! You absolute coward!' Sam sat for over an hour trying to persuade his brother to come with him. Finally, Honey agreed to go, but only if Sam got him a 'Noble Steed'.

Sam went out immediately to find Honey a horse, but the horses had all been taken by the King in preparation for battle. He stood in the middle of a street racking his brains and trying to think what to do. Honey would settle for nothing but a horse! *Or will he?* thought Sam, as he saw a cat riding a white Donkey. The cat was quick to agree to sell the donkey to Sam for a high price.

'Oh Sam! It's a beautiful Noble Steed. Thanks awfully.' It had worked! Honey was convinced that it was a grand war horse. 'What's his noble name, Sammaramus?'

'Balaam.'

'And such a noble name!' Honey stroked the donkey's nose.

'Tomorrow we set out to find Tenga!' said Sam, fingering the commission ring in his pocket.

Chapter 8

A Meeting with Darkness

Sam and Honey descended slowly into a valley, the horse and donkey struggling to keep their footing on the loose stones of the deep descent. Balaam the donkey finally gave in to the stones and he and Honey found themselves rolling and sliding rapidly to the bottom, where they splashed into the deep blue waters of the river below.

'Honey-buns! You alright?' asked Sam as he

dragged the soaked Honey to shore.

'Yeah, fine. You see, my clever steed realised the quickest way down and took it. He has the same brilliance of brains as myself...well, almost.' Honey shook himself to try and dry himself, but failed by reason of the light armour and clothes.

'No one can doubt it…that horse *almost* condescends to your brains.'

Honey wasn't too sure what 'condescend' meant, but assumed that it was a positive word and smiled and nodded his head in his happy ignorance.

'Well, now we've got to the river we have to go alongside it until we get to the bridge that leads straight to the Gronad's lair.' Sam mounted his black horse after helping Honey back onto the donkey.

'One question, Sammy m'boy: why is this dragon called a Gronad?'

'The name "Gronad" is simply the letters of the word "dragon" all mixed around. We call him the Gronad to stop the very young animals realising that there is such a thing as a dragon.'

Evening soon set in and the dying embers of the sun shone out and lit up the valley ahead of them with a kind of innocent brilliance. The river was tinted with pink and gold like some enchanted road leading onwards, beyond the view to the never-worlds. Sam's eyes followed the river to the horizon and there saw a bridge silhouetted against the sinking sun.

'That's the bridge, Honey! Get ready for some excitement; we'll be at the entrance to the Gronad's cave by dark!'

The bridge seemed to get bigger and bigger as they approached it. By the time they stood at the first golden step it was almost as big as the palace back in Gilland.

'Wow! Just how big is this Gronad thing, Sammaramus?'

'The largest and most vicious creature in the whole of our world.'

'What was that, Sammy? I think I must have misheard you or something; did you say "vicious"?'

'Of course. It's a dragon. Dragons are supposed to be big and vicious!'

'Oh. Well, I think I have an appointment with someone very important back in Gilland. Good luck with the dragon, Sam!' Honey smiled sweetly and turned his donkey's head back the way they had come.

'No Honey! You're coming with me, you coward!'

'I'm no coward, I just have perfectly rational

fears of things that are fearful...' He knew he had to obey Sam, though, so he sighed and turned back to the foot of the golden bridge. He tried to look sick, hoping Sam would let him go back to Gilland on the grounds that he was far too ill to cope with such an enterprise. However, he found it impossible to make his face pale; instead, it went a reddish colour with the effort.

Sam ignored Honey as he nudged his horse on to the first step of the bridge. Sam reached out and slowly brushed his paw along the wall of the bridge. It felt smooth and cold.

'Pure gold,' he muttered under his breath.

'It's not fair is it, Balaam?' said Honey. 'I mean, our rights are being ignored here. Why shouldn't we go back to Gilland? We should make a stand for our rights. He's just a rash and stupid young dog!'

With many more such complaints, Honey rode on, keeping far enough behind Sam so as he would not hear him.

'Hang on, what's that smell?'

Honey raised his muzzle and sniffed the air; he smelt burning and an indescribably horrible stench. He turned around to face a terrifying, black, four-legged creature lunging towards them. He shouted frantically to Sam for help, just as the creature leaped right over both of them and stopped in the middle of the bridge, blocking their path.

Even Sam trembled as he looked at the hideous thing. It was deformed beyond description and its eyes were blood red. It grinned as thunder clouds formed in the skies above. Its teeth were like two rows of sharp knives, the yellowy colour of them contrasting sharply with its black body and red eyes.

Sam and Honey were frozen with fright, Sam's paw resting uselessly on the hilt of his sword.

It grew very dark, but Sam could just make out the figure of the creature pacing in a circle in front of them; constantly watching them, constantly grinning at them. Eventually it stopped, sat quietly down, raised its head and gave a cry that was half screech and half scream. Suddenly, a thunderbolt of lightning zigzagged down from the skies and lit up the bridge just where the creature was sitting. The creature was gone and the bridge began to melt.

'Quick Honey, back the way we came!' Sam turned his horse around and, with the horse bucking and shying at almost every pace, they made it to the river bank just as the beautiful bridge collapsed and disappeared in the raging water. The two wet and bedraggled dogs hurried to the woods nearby and climbed a huge sturdy tree.

'We shall have to keep hidden up here Honey, it's not safe where that…thing might get us.'

'Well, Sammaramous, I'm not a bird or a squirrel or a rabbit, but I'm just as clever as they and I suppose I can work out how to sleep in a tree.' Honey snuggled down on the crook of a branch, then turned to Sam again. 'Rabbits live in trees don't they, Sam?'

'No, rabbits live in the ground! Go to sleep Honey!'

'I'm sure you're wrong, Sam, rabbits do live in trees. I can prove it to you: I say they live in trees and I'm always right, so there!' With that they both fell into a deep sleep.

CRACK, CRASH, THUMP!!

'Honey, are you alright?' Sam looked anxiously down on the fallen yellow dog on the ground. Honey got up and rubbed his sleepy eyes with his paws, which is quite a hard feat for dogs.

'I must have fallen out the tree,' Honey shouted back up to Sam, who was laughing uncontrollably.

'I can see that!'

'Do you reckon rabbits fall out of trees in the morning and that's why they are always up so early?' asked Honey as he started putting his armour on.

'Rabbits don't live in trees!' Sam climbed nimbly down and gathered wood to cook breakfast.

'Of course they do, haven't you ever seen a rabbit fall out of a tree?'

'No.' Sam put two fishes on the fire.

'Well I have…I think.'

Suddenly they heard a rustling in the bushes and the crack of a branch underfoot. Sam looked around but could see nothing.

'I think we better forget about breakfast and move on, Honey,' whispered Sam. 'I think every move we take is being watched by that creature. The other side of the river is far too steep for us to just swim or boat across. We shall have to take a raft or something downstream. Quickly now, get as many logs and things as you can. I learned how to make a raft extra fast when I was a squire.'

Indeed, they were quick at the job and soon all, including the horses, were packed onto the sturdy-looking raft. Sam untied it, shoved it towards the middle of the river and jumped on. The main current picked up the vessel and soon they were floating along at a fast but comfortable pace. Sam kept scanning the river bank. He could have sworn that he saw a dark shadow every so often, stealthily moving parallel to them, but concluded that it was his imagination.

The river went on and on in a dead straight line, leading them towards the unknown. Sam's nerves were tensing; everything seemed so unnatural.

'What do you reckon that black… smelly… red-eyed thing was, Sammy?'

'I don't know, Honey, but it was the same creature that burned the tree that could have given us the clue to finding Tenga. Whatever it is, it doesn't want us to find the little leopard.'

'Do you think it was Lord Mould?'

'No, Lord Mould doesn't look like that, but it's very similar.' Sam steered the raft a little further away from the river bank.

'Perhaps a distant relative, Sam.' Honey smiled and lay back further on the provisions and blankets. He sighed contentedly as he realised just how clever he was to come to such a brilliant conclusion. 'What does Lord Mould look like?'

'Can't really say to tell you the truth. Dad saw him once – he's the only one – and said that he was tall and horrible beyond telling. The only real feature he could talk about was Lord Mould's eyes…' Sam looked away to the horizon.

'Out with it then, Sam.'

'His eyes are like raging fires and ashes. When Dad looked into them he saw the burning of his childhood farm, which came to pass.'

Honey shuddered and changed the topic of conversation to other important matters, like the new song he was composing. That subject exhausted, he talked about the picture he was going to draw as soon as they got back to Gilland. He talked on non-stop about this and that, not missing out his favourite subject of how clever he was. Sam just listened and thought to himself. *I can't help thinking that this river was made for a purpose, to lead unwary travellers to a certain place.*

Honey was soon snoozing at the back of the raft, as the afternoon brought on grey, clouded skies and a few drops of light rain.

Suddenly, the current got steadily quicker and quicker until it was carrying the raft onwards at a startling speed. It was drawing them towards a black mass of fog up ahead. Sam desperately tried to steer the raft to shore, but the helm just moved independently of the raft.

'What's going on, Honey, are you messing around with the steering?' But Honey was still asleep. Sam looked around for a way of drawing the raft back to the bank, but they were soon engulfed in the thick black fog. The fog felt thick and damp and all was pitch black and deathly quiet.

Sam could hear and feel his heart thump hard against his chest, his throat felt suddenly dry and tight. He drew out his sword, and then he saw it – two flames of fire appeared in the darkness and came closer. He could feel an icy breath of wind and smelt burning and that stench again. His eyes were drawn to the two flames of fire and he saw in them the whole of Gilland in flames.

'Lord Mould!' he said in a thin whisper.

Chapter 9

In the Underworld

Sam stared into Lord Mould's eyes, unable to draw himself away from their gaze.

'Honey!' he cried, pulling himself away. 'Get your sword and fight!'

Honey was finally aroused from his slumber and quickly got up and drew his sword. His expression changed from sleepiness to a kind of curious and almost comfortable look. The fiery eyes turned their gaze away from Sam to Honey, and Honey smiled when he saw them. Then the eyes vanished. Sam noticed that the red half of Honey's left eye was glowing like embers in the dark.

Suddenly they were grabbed from behind and dragged through a hole in the side of the river bank nearest the Gronad. They could see nothing of their capturer but heard his gruff voice.

'Never go anywhere near that fog. It would kill you.'

The gruff-voiced animal lit a torch and Sam and Honey found themselves face to face with a one-eyed badger.

'Sam,' whispered Honey, 'are badgers good guys or bad guys?' He was trembling.

'Oh, you may as well say that we are on your side if you are not on Lord Mould's side,' said the badger. 'Excuse me.' They squeezed past three young rabbits who were idly discussing whether they should go out for a stroll or not.

'Notice the rabbits, Honey?' Sam had a half-smile on his face.

'Still doesn't mean that rabbits don't live in trees. Perhaps these ones have just decided to take on badger nationality.' Honey stuck his muzzle in the air.

'May as well come to my home and talk. You

seem pretty ignorant animals. Travelling are you?' The badger seemed friendly enough, but Honey *would* lecture him on how he was by no means ignorant.

'In fact you would be surprised at my surpassing knowledge... That is the right use of 'surpassing' isn't it Sam?' Honey babbled on and on; and the passages went on and on, just like the passages under the prison in Clawland. They were crowded with underground animals of all sorts, from foxes to mice, all lounging around or talking about nothing in particular.

Eventually they stopped at a door and the badger fumbled around in one of his pockets for his key. Inside it was cozy and warm; it felt very safe. They sat down in comfortable armchairs around a glowing coal fire.

'Now tell me your story,' said the old badger.

Sam told of their adventures up until the description of Lord Mould's eyes, when Honey chipped in.

'Oh that was Lord Mould, was it?'

'Yes, Honey, didn't you realise?' Sam looked curiously at Honey.

'No. I expected it to be a scary experience, but it was beautiful.' Honey smiled.

'What's your account of the meeting with Lord

Mould, then?' the badger asked Honey.

'I woke up from a comfortable dream and was stunned by a goldish light. It seemed that my right eye and half of my left eye saw nothing, but the red half of my left eye saw everything. I saw pleasant groves with plump red grapes ready to be harvested. I was going to reach out to pick a bunch but my attention was drawn to a hideous being. I wasn't afraid of it though, in fact I pitied it. It looked at me with fiery red eyes that looked like the cosy fires that we had at my house on those snowy cold winter days…'

'Stop!' cried the badger. 'This is very strange indeed. Why do you have that red in your left eye?'

'He had an accident when he was a young pup,' said Sam. 'My dad told me about it. That eye never quite healed and he's half blind in it.'

The badger did not look convinced, but changed the topic to more general talk.

'We are having a feast tonight, all the Underworld animals will be there. It's a grand gathering and you are quite welcome to join us. It's not often that we get outsiders, or Overworld animals.'

'Of course we'll come,' said Sam. 'But you haven't told me your name yet, or anything about you and this…Underworld place.'

'My name is Ridge. My story is pretty simple. I grew up with my family in this place and, like all the animals here, I ate and drank and didn't bother myself with work, battles and adventure like you folk up there...'

'What a boring life!' Honey blurted out, and Sam shot him a warning glance that told him to shut up.

'I dreamed of adventure, but that's not something that an Underworlder can do without having dishonour attached to his name.' Ridge scratched his nose with his long powerful claws. 'As for this place, we make our living by forcing slaves to mine jewels and coal to sell to the Overworlders. We banquet every other night and laze about during the day. The more ambitious rabbits sometimes go to work for the Great Eagle, but that's a sad business.'

'I visited the Great Eagle once,' said Sam. 'I noticed the rabbits and wondered a lot about them. Why are they there?'

'They volunteer. But when they get there they find that the Great Eagle is a hard master and treats them badly if they step out of place. There are rumours also as to where the Eagle gets its food, but they are only rumours and we should leave them at that.'

Honey shuddered. 'He's evil then?'

'Some say he is, some say he's not. It's hard to tell. Sometimes the Eagle does noble and heroic things for other animals,' said Ridge. 'But at the end of the day, he's the only one we can look to for protection against Lord Mould. The Great Eagle and Lord Mould are mortal enemies. They are always fighting. Sometimes one wins and sometimes the other wins. They would do anything to harm each other or anything connected with each other. Ah, I think it's time we went to the feast.'

They were soon walking along those endless passages and turnings.

'It's a wonder that they don't get lost!' said Honey.

They finally reached the great hall, where the banquet had already started. The hall was massive and perfectly round. It was cut a little deeper into the ground and steps lined the inside, much like Greek amphitheatres. Honey rushed down to get to the food, tripped on one of the stairs and found himself rolling and crashing straight into one of the tables. The animals at the table were much amused by it and soon Honey was messing around and enjoying himself thoroughly.

Sam and Ridge walked to the other, more sober,

side of the banqueting hall, and sat down at a table with badgers and foxes. Sam recognised the fox that sat opposite him; its blackish red coat was easy to distinguish anywhere. It was the Clawlandite fox that acted as a spy for King Farratol. He immediately engaged it in conversation.

'Why are you here?' he asked.

'I always stop here for the banquets on my way to Clawland. I was brought up here before I joined the Clawlandite army, you see,' said the fox.

'What do you do in Clawland?' Sam bit into a leg of turkey.

'I'm the assistant to Lord Mould now, a very useful role for gathering information about his planned attack on Gilland.'

'Why do you play chess with the King so much? Surely you have more important things to talk about?'

The fox laughed. 'I'll tell you about the chess game. Before Lord Mould became what he is, he was so fond of chess that he played it all the time and became world champion.'

'So Lord Mould wasn't always a mouldy rotting creature?' Sam interrupted.

'No, he was an animal once. He became what he is because of greed and self conceitedness. It consumed him. He won a number of battles with the Great Eagle and doted on himself and his spoils ever after. He was the gentlest animal of all in his youth. But something changed him. Some say it was guilt – a guilt he couldn't cope with and he blamed others so much for.'

The fox paused while he took a swig from his tankard. 'But about the chess game – at the moment Lord Mould has all the positions and moves of the divisions of his army planned out for the battle. He's set it up like a chess game and will stick to the plan through thick and thin. Now, I have been getting information of his plan – his chess game – and have been passing the information on to the King. We then sit down and play chess. I play Lord Mould's side and he plays Gilland's side. If he can find a way of defeating me in the chess game, then he can place the divisions of his army according to the pieces on the board and, hopefully, the battle will go exactly according to the chess game. Thus Gilland would win. The only problem is killing Lord Mould. If he lives on he will just wage war again and again until Gilland is exhausted. Only his bloodline can kill him.'

'That's simple then!' said Sam with a clearer expression on his face. 'We find Lord Mould's son and persuade him to fight for us.'

'Lord Mould never had a son.' The Clawlandite

fox looked grave. 'You don't realise the seriousness of this matter. I've gathered all the information I could get for the King, but still no plan of action has been made. On top of this, there are rumours that Lord Mould has created a deadly pet that will do his command whatever the circumstances.'

'Well, they say the only real hope is if we find Tenga,' Sam sighed. 'But who knows where on earth to find a quiet little leopard cub? We're heading towards the Gronad at the moment.'

'The Gronad is a good place to start at any rate, but he's more dangerous than you think. And he's awfully stupid.'

'Basically, we're lost at the moment. We have no idea how to find the Gronad's cave from here.'

Ridge, who had been listening all this time, spoke up. 'I'll guide you to the Gronad. He's not far from here.'

'My path goes that way too. We better set off immediately,' said the Clawlandite fox, rising from the table. 'By the way, my name's Trussatismatis, but you can call me Truss for short. My mother liked the Clawlandite name Trussatismatis, but it was too long for my friends to remember. The Underworlders were in alliance with Clawland at one stage.'

Ridge coughed and changed the subject. 'Where's Syrup gone?'

'I think you mean Honey,' Sam smiled.

'Yes. Honey. Ah, there he is, entertaining everyone with a song.'

It was too true. Honey was standing on the table and singing as loud as he could, while the other animals were clapping along to it. The song was as ridiculous as usual and it went something like this.

'I like the Underworld, and I want to stay here forever,
'Cause you all have fun
And my name is Hon
-ey, and I am so clever!'

Sam rushed up and dragged Honey out into the passages. Suddenly they heard a loud screech.

'Lord Mould's pet!' cried Truss and they began to run as fast as they could along the tunnels. Ridge pulled open a door and ushered them into the dark inside, slamming the door behind them. Honey fell against some sharp stones and cried out.

'Hush! Be quiet!' Sam whispered. Then they heard the creature sniffing the bottom of the door.

Chapter 10

The End of the World

Lord Mould's pet paced around outside the door for a few minutes, but it seemed like an eternity to Sam and Honey. Then all was quiet again. Ridge lit a torch and the rays revealed that the sharp stones piled up behind their backs were, in fact, jewels of various kinds. They were in a store-room.

'These are some of the goods we mine in this place. This is where all our riches come from,' said

Ridge, as he picked up a diamond and brushed the dust off. 'We don't get as much business these days though.'

Honey quietly and slowly took a handful of jewels and put them into his pocket. They stayed in the hold all night and found it extremely uncomfortable to sleep.

However, sleep they did and, before they knew it, morning had arrived.

'Well, we must be moving on,' said Sam. 'I think Lord Mould's pet is gone. It must have been the creature that Honey and I saw the other night – the one that destroyed the Golden Bridge.'

'So Lord Mould doesn't want you to get to the Gronad,' mused Truss. 'Very interesting.'

'Must mean that the Gronad has Tenga, so we're on the right track.' Sam got up and opened the door. He looked all around but could see nothing of Lord Mould's pet.

They followed Ridge through more endless tunnels until they began to see a spot of light at the end of one. The light grew bigger and bigger. The old badger stopped at the exit and sniffed the air.

'This is the opening. I ordered a few young rabbits and mice to bring your horses and provisions here.'

As they stepped out into the open the light

blinded them for a second, for they had become so accustomed to the dim lighting of the Underworld. As soon as Honey's eyes adjusted he saw Balaam and ran to him. He flung his paws around him and hugged him until the donkey was almost blue in the face.

'My dear Noble Steed! I've so missed you. You weren't afraid of Lord Mould, were you?'

Honey put his armour on and saddled his donkey. The fox mounted his chestnut horse and Ridge was waiting on his black and white horse. Soon they were all ready to go. Sam felt a lot more confident now that he was back in the saddle. He had been trained to fight on horseback and felt uncomfortable on the ground.

'Just over this range of mountains,' said Ridge pointing to the snow-capped mountains up ahead of them, 'you'll find the Gronad's den. Truss and I will go with you until we get to the small village on the other side of that mountain straight ahead.'

'Alright,' said Sam, 'you stay there until our safe return with Tenga and you can come back with us to Gilland in triumph!'

'I wouldn't be so sure,' said Truss, who seemed to have a permanent air of apprehension about him.

Honey started singing one of the Gillandite

nursery rhymes as they began the ascent up the mountain. It was a rhyme about a snake that tied itself into a huge knot because it was so conceited that it kept hugging and admiring itself. The horses were soon tired out from climbing and the riders from listening to Honey singing so they stopped on a ledge to rest.

'Look at that scenery, Sammaramus,' cried Honey, wagging his tail with pleasure. 'You can see everything. It kind of makes me want to write a poem. Got any paper?'

Sam gave Honey a pen and paper and soon he was covered in ink and surrounded by scrunched-up pieces of paper.

Sam scanned the open countryside. Indeed, it was a sight to behold! They could see lush green grasslands on their side of the river with cattle and sheep grazing on it, so small that they looked like little wooden toys. On the other side of the dead straight river, right ahead of them, the forest stretched out to the horizon, every so often meeting a bald patch which would show a town or village. Right on the horizon was another mountain range and, on the top of the highest mountain, was nested the golden castle of the Great Eagle.

The northern mountain range stretched towards

the east and around in a semi-circle to connect to the mountain range they were on. These two mountain ranges lined the edge of all land, and beyond them was the sea that surrounded the land and dropped in magnificent waterfalls off the edge of the world.

To the far left, the mountain ranges broke away from each other and left a gap where the beautiful white city of Gilland perched next to the vast crystal sea. Sam could make out his own country and his heart throbbed with home sickness.

He turned his gaze away to the right where the forest stopped suddenly and gave way to scorched wastelands with burned trees and grass. In between where the two mountain ranges met was the City of Clawland, and Lord Mould's castle towering like a menace on the side of a mountain just above.

'We had better move on,' said Ridge, 'so that we can get to the village by nightfall.'

They were now near the top of the mountain. It was deep with snow and very cold. Sam wrapped his cloak tighter around him as they pressed on at a slow pace. After a laborious climb they reached the top of the mountain and Sam and Honey were delighted to see the great sea stretching before them.

'Sam, look!' Honey was pointing to near the

horizon, hardly able to keep still with excitement. 'There's the end of the world!'

Indeed it was. They could even hear the roar of the massive waterfalls from where they were standing and see the stunningly colourful rainbows crowning the top of them.

'I've been to the four corners of the world,' breathed Sam. 'Gilland of the west, Clawland of the east, the Great Eagle's castle of the north, and this mountain at the south. And now I've seen the end of the world.'

They had to draw themselves away from staring at the end of the world and press on down the other side of the mountain. It was not long before the snow gave way to flowery grasslands and there was the village, made of garnet stones from the mines.

The animals spoke a different language and were dressed in strange garments. The food was different, too. They were the Endworlders. Fortunately, Ridge and Truss knew the language and culture, so Sam and Honey were able to relax.

Honey found out how to get himself surrounded by Endworlders and sung song after song until late into the night. He sung around the fire and some ventured to join in. Not knowing the language meant that they had to imitate the sounds of the words that Honey was making, which amused the fun-loving yellow dog very much, and he began to think that this quest wasn't so bad after all. He did get tired of singing about four hours before sunrise and went to bed in one of the little garnet cottages. Both dogs were full of adventure, however, and they couldn't get to sleep.

'What's over the edge of the world, Sammy?' Honey asked, sitting up on his sheepskin bed.

'Lot's of strange worlds with strange creatures. Beyond that is a new universe with lots of wasted planets and only one with living things on it.'

'What's that planet like?'

'The atmosphere and landscape is much like ours but a lot bigger. But believe it or not, that world is not flat like ours, but round!' Sam gave a little laugh as the fact always tickled him.

'Round!' Honey sat bolt upright and his eyes grew wide. 'Then all they can do is go around and around and never find a place to stop.'

'Perhaps, but the strangest thing is the creatures that live on the planet. They have animals like us, but they're more like horses and donkeys and livestock – they can't speak or think, wear clothes, live in their own houses, have Kings, or battles. All those things are taken by a race superior to any that's been known – humans. They are so clever that they have made non-living things move without touching them. They've made them do things for them.'

Honey sighed. 'I'd like to go and explore a new world one day, and I'd take Balaam with me.'

'These other worlds have never been proven of course, just rumours and speculations. Anyway, how could a planet be round? It wouldn't be able to float!' said Sam. 'But before you go to sleep, Honey, I think you had better give me those jewels that you stole from the Underworld store.'

'How did you know I stole them?' Honey asked.

'I saw one fall out of your pocket.'

Honey sighed and gave Sam the jewels. For the next hour Sam lectured Honey on the evils of stealing, until Honey got bored and fell asleep.

I shan't forget to return these to Ridge tomorrow, thought Sam as he lay back on his pillow and slipped into a sound sleep.

'Get up! You have to go to the Gronad and get all this bad business over.' Ridge was shaking Sam awake.

'Right!' said Sam, getting his armour on and saddling his horse. He could hear loud snoring from Honey.

'I think you had better try and get Syrup up,'

said Ridge. 'I've been trying the last half hour with various means, including the bucket of water, but he's a sound sleeper in the truest sense of the word.'

'His name is Honey, not Syrup,' said Sam going over to Honey. 'I know how to wake him up.' Sam whispered the word 'Breakfast' and Honey was soon up and eating that word.

After that they rode away with Ridge's encouragement and Truss' warnings. Ridge had directed them to follow the road around the side of the mountain and then drop down into the valley between the present mountain and its neighbour.

The valley didn't look too bad. It was rather wide and the sand was soft on the horse's and donkey's hooves, enabling them to go cautiously and quietly. But then the valley narrowed right down to the breadth of two horses, so they had to go in single file, with Sam at the front, to avoid scraping their stirrups against the rock faces of the two mountains. The ground became rocky, too, and the horse's and donkey's hooves echoed eerily around the mountains. There was no other sound, no other living creature or plant, and the huge mountains began to obscure the sun so that they were in cold shadows.

Honey shivered. 'This place don't look too friendly!'

Sam pulled up his horse as the valley ended at the entrance of a huge cave. They could see a glow inside that brightened and dimmed like a heave of breath, again and again. Honey coughed as the entrance issued out smoke that stung their nostrils and lungs.

'I must be brave, I must be brave,' muttered Honey to himself, shaking all over.

Chapter 11

The Gronad

The dim light in the cave grew as the Gronad approached the entrance. A deafening roar shook the stones and rocks. Sam and Honey trembled and gripped their poised swords tighter as they heard a tremendous sound of the beating of massive wings. They heard the beast take in a deep breath. Fire and an immense heat bellowed forth from the mouth of the cave. Then it came in sight:

a fearful creature, five times the size of an elephant, crawled along the ground on thin front legs and large powerful back legs. It clawed the rock face and its iron-like claws made four neat furrows in the rock. Its head was small but its jaws and green eyes were large. Two columns of smoke came from its nostrils and a fire deep inside its powerful body lit it up and made its tightly fitted scales glow a hot red.

'Right, Balaam! Here goes!' cried Honey, as his donkey reared like a horse. 'Charge!'

Honey held out his sword with his right paw, the sharp tip pointed towards the Gronad, his other paw holding the reins. In the height of both Honey and Balaam's excitement, the Gronad just stared at them with those big green eyes.

Suddenly Balaam came to a skidding stop and Honey was hard put to keep in the saddle and not fly over the donkey's head. With a gleam in his eyes, Balaam trotted off to the right to a pile of carrots. After all, he hadn't had carrots in such a long time and they could easily fight this big red monster after he had finished his lunch. Besides, he needed the energy: that charge was more than he had done in a long time. Thoughts such as these passed through Honey's 'Noble Steed' while nibbling at the delicious carrots. Honey wasn't too bothered about the whole carrot issue either. He'd much rather leave the fighting to Sam.

'You cowards! Both of you!' Sam shouted at Honey. 'You never come to my help when I need you. You just come along for all the fun and games.'

But his attention was diverted back to the Gronad, who was pawing the ground again. A low grumble of impatience issued from its terrible mouth. Sam made his horse canter slightly sideways towards the Gronad to put himself in a better fighting position and not have to wield his sword over the horse's head.

The Gronad blew a line of fire at the black knight, but Sam's horse managed to jump over it. The Gronad was furious and clapped his wings together. He approached Sam and swung his tail, which was as big and strong as a fir tree, at Strawberry. The horse was knocked hard into the wall from right underneath Sam, but Sam was just quick enough to jump onto the Gronad's tail and stab his golden sword deep into it. Sam knew that the only tender place on the Gronad was its tail, just like any puppy. The Gronad wriggled and writhed in pain and threw Sam heavily on the ground, where he lay still.

'Sam!' Honey cried, waving his sword at the

Gronad. 'You beast, you killed my little brother! When I come back I will kill you!'

He jumped onto his donkey and galloped madly off, not heeding which direction he was going. Tears of rage stung his cheeks but he galloped on. He came to the seashore and galloped along it until the sun sank below the same waterfall that had fascinated him and his brother just the other day.

He finally stopped and lay down on the grass next to the beach. The world suddenly felt so big and empty and lonely, and he felt lost in it. He had never imagined a time when he wouldn't have Sam to guide him and protect him. He began to realise how dependent he was on his little brother. His eyes were sore and red from crying, and he had to rest them. He was soon fast asleep on the edge of the world, all alone.

In the morning his mind was a little bit clearer, although his heart still ached, and he tried to think what to do next. He had never had to think wholly for himself, and he spent until noon thinking and staring at the sea, while Balaam grazed quite peacefully. Finally he decided he would get up and find his way back to Ridge and Truss. He could see the mountain off to his right and a little behind him. He stood up and shook the dew out of his fur and clothes. Then he began to saddle Balaam.

'That's funny,' he said to Balaam. 'I'm sure it was sunny just now.' Indeed, a shadow had fallen on them, but it was not a cloud. Honey looked up and his eyes grew large with terror. The Great Eagle from the other side of the world was swooping down on him with its sharp talons outstretched,

'I have you now, Honey,' it said. 'I've hunted the world to find you at a convenient moment to kill you.'

'Sam, help!' he shouted, but there was no Sam to come to his rescue now. The Eagle dug his talons into Honey's back and he screamed with pain. But just as the Great Eagle swooped down for the last attack, a hideous rider covered in mould galloped towards them like the wind. It drew out a long mouldy sword and attacked the Great Eagle.

'Leave that dog alone,' said Lord Mould. His voice was like a whisper that echoed through the mountain like a sweet memory lost. The Great Eagle and Lord Mould fought viciously.

'Go, Honey,' said Lord Mould, fixing his fiery eyes on the confused dog. One look in Lord Mould's eyes comforted Honey immediately, though he only saw him with half of his left eye, and he calmly mounted Balaam and rode off to find Ridge and Truss.

'Where's Sam?' asked Ridge.

'The Gronad killed him.' Honey had made it safely back to the Endworld village.

'You look tired, you should get some rest,' said Ridge. 'And I had better see to that wound on your back.'

Accordingly, Honey slept the whole afternoon and woke up with a start. 'I must go and revenge myself.'

'Are you mad? You can't kill the Gronad!' said Truss.

'I have to. Besides, it would make a good song to sing about afterwards – *The Revenge of Honey*.' He stepped outside and breathed in the fresh air. He was determined.

He took six confident steps down the road and remembered the Gronad's claws, so he ran back to the cottage and locked the door. Ridge and Truss smiled to each other. Honey breathed deeply a few times then opened the door again and stepped out. He was not afraid - he was going to avenge Sam.

This time he made five confident steps and remembered the Gronad's jaws. He was soon in the cottage again with the door locked. This performance was repeated a number of times until the whole anatomy of the Gronad had been thought about and Honey decided that he would do the job another day when he had more time.

In the evening he was persuaded by the Endworlders to sing and play games with them, which he did every night for a whole week. Each night he would tell them some detail about his 'heroic' encounter with the Gronad, and each night the story would get more and more unbelievable and dramatic, until he was describing how he killed the Gronad with one powerful blow from his sword.

During the day he would entertain himself as much as possible with this and that, including writing poems and songs and drawing pictures for the Endworlders. Eventually, every animal in the village had one of Honey's drawings or paintings and he grew very popular.

In such manner a week went by. One evening, as Honey was sitting on the porch of the cottage writing a song about the sun arguing with the moon, he saw a very familiar figure walking slowly along the road towards him.

Chapter 12

Sam's Tale

'SAM!' Honey cried. He jumped up and spilt ink all over himself, then ran full speed at Sam and knocked him over. 'What have you been getting up to with that Gronad, Sam?' Honey pulled Sam to his feet and dusted him down.

'That's rather a long story, Honey. I'll tell you all about it after I've had my dinner. Did Strawberry come back?'

'No, Strawberry's not here. Perhaps he trotted off somewhere to get some carrots.' Honey turned around to run back to the house and tell Truss and the badger that Sam was home.

Sam stopped him. 'What happened to you Honey? Your cloak is all torn.'

'Oh, that was from the Great Eagle. He attacked me and scratched my back. It's almost better now.'

'The Great Eagle?' Sam looked curiously at Honey and remembered the tapestry. 'How did you get away?'

'Well…I…I just did.' Honey quickly looked away from Sam and then ran to the house.

Something's up with that dog! thought Sam. *He's either hiding something or afraid to tell.*

He followed Honey into the house and was greeted with joy by Ridge and a bleak 'I told you that you were no match for the Gronad' by Truss. He sat down at the table and they ate and talked quite happily. After dinner, Sam pushed back his chair and began his story. This is what happened to him:

When Sam was knocked into the rock face he merely lost consciousness. When Honey left him, he was picked up by the Gronad and gently carried in his mouth into the cave. He was a curious animal and was keen to learn more about the strange knight that had wanted to kill him. He was a peaceful animal overall, despite being a dragon, and it was his principle not to eat others until he found out everything interesting about them. Then he could enjoy eating them all the more. It was much like how some animals back in Gilland loved to know the exact ingredients of their food before they ate it.

The Gronad took Sam deep into the heart of the mountain, where it was boiling hot, and waited for him to wake up. The first thing Sam saw when he opened his eyes was a pair of large round green eyes staring curiously at him. He jumped up and whistled for Strawberry, but his black horse was gone.

'So, are you going to eat me then?' Sam asked, not expecting a reply. He only said it in frustration.

'When I feel like it,' the Gronad replied. His throaty voice was half a growl and half a purr.

Sam stared at the dragon. 'You can talk?'

'Why shouldn't I? You are allowed to talk.'

'Of course.' Sam was keen to keep the peace. 'Why shouldn't you talk, you look quite smart.'

'You think so?' the Gronad grinned, showing his knife-like teeth. 'I think so too.'

You're just like Honey! thought Sam. *Perhaps I can deal with you.*

'Please, black dog thing,' asked the Gronad, 'can you take your thorn out of my tail?'

'Thorn?'

The Gronad swung his tail around and Sam realised that he meant his sword.

'That's the sword my dad gave me.' He yanked it out and was almost shocked to see big boiling teardrops drip down the Gronad's face. 'Surely it's not that painful!'

'I can't stand pain,' said the Gronad.

Sam began to find the whole situation rather comical, ignoring the fact that he was probably about to be this wimp's dinner. 'My name's Sam, by the way.'

'You're from Gilland then?'

Sam nodded.

'A simple Gillandite name. I remember eating a number of Gillandites, but they're a delicacy in these parts,' said the Gronad.

'Should I be worried by that comment?' asked Sam, raising his eyebrows.

'Depends whether you like being eaten or not.'

'Never tried it.' Sam was fed up with messing around and got straight to the point. 'Have you got Tenga here?'

The Gronad was beginning to like the calm Sam. He was tired of the usual screaming and escaping animals that he usually caught, so he was willing to oblige. 'What animal might Tenga be then?'

'A young cute leopard, very quiet.' Sam's heart beat faster as he waited for the reply.

The Gronad scratched its small head with its back leg. 'I had to go and get a leopard cub from a camp near the Great Eagle once. I had it here for a little while.'

Sam's heart skipped a beat. 'Who told you to get the leopard?'

'The Great Eagle did. He told me to bring it to Lord Mould as soon as possible with a message saying that the cub was a gift and he looked forward to the battle.' The Gronad yawned and fiddled with a piece of gold.

The Great Eagle! thought Sam. *Why would he want Lord Mould to destroy Gilland?*

'Is Tenga safe?' he asked.

'I don't know. I think Lord Mould had some purpose for him because he wouldn't let me harm him. I just dropped the little thing off at Clawland. Wouldn't have made much of a meal anyway.' The Gronad sighed. 'I'm tired of this game, Sam. I think I'll have dinner now.' He bared his teeth.

'No, I wouldn't do that!' Sam was panting, half from the heat and half from nervousness.

'Why?' the Gronad was suddenly interested.

'Because…look,' Sam reached into his pocket to take out the commission ring. Instead, he felt the jewels Honey had stolen and took them out. *Must have forgotten to give these back to Ridge,* he thought. *Oh well, they may just do the trick.*

Then he said, 'I'll give you these to build up your collection…' Sam looked at a tiny pile of gold and jewels in the corner of the cave, '…if you promise not to eat me.'

The Gronad's eyes grew bigger and rounder, if that were possible.

'Oh, thank you! They're lovely!' He took the jewels greedily from Sam and chuckled to himself.

Stupid creature! thought Sam, as he waited patiently until the Gronad finally stopped gloating over the jewels.

'I promise not to eat you, Sam. In fact, you can be a guest in my cave as long as you like.' The Gronad gently laid the jewels with the rest of his collection.

This dragon and Honey could be brothers, they're so alike! thought Sam.

Later that evening Sam found himself in the bizarre situation of playing chess with a very temperamental dragon. He had to let the Gronad win every game or else the beast would get so angry. While they were playing their fourth game, he remembered the conversation with Truss about the forthcoming battle and the King playing chess. *What a world we live in!*

'Tomorrow you must come with me for a fly around,' said the Gronad.

'Splendid idea,' said Sam. But he thought differently: he knew time was running out and they needed to find Tenga. Nevertheless, next morning he was out on the beach climbing onto the Gronad's back. Once Sam finally managed to get onto the huge dragon, the Gronad stretched his wings and leaped into the air. He flapped his wings majestically as they soared up to the heavens.

'This is great!' said Sam, clutching onto the Gronad with the wind whipping his face. He looked down to see the mountains and the whole world again. They flew up above the clouds and Sam was fascinated to see the clouds below stretched out like a landscape of their own. It looked so pure and inviting. *What fun it would be to walk around on those clouds as if they were land!* thought Sam.

'Now, I'll show you my favourite view.' The Gronad was delighted to see Sam enjoying the flight. Only once before had he befriended another animal, and that was Tenga, though he wouldn't admit it to Sam.

They gradually descended back down through the clouds, just above the sea. The Gronad took Sam right to the edge of the world – to the waterfall. The sound was deafening and the spray came up and soaked Sam all over. *I'm wet with water that comes from outside the world!* he mused.

Then he was struck with an overwhelming sense of awe, as the Gronad flew beyond the waterfall and Sam looked down to see the water crashing down on an atmosphere surrounding an oval red planet far below. He gazed down to see planets of all different shapes and sizes and colours. He even spotted a perfectly round one! He saw suns and moons and stars. He saw galaxies and the black holes like tiny dots in the distance that went from their universe to other universes. He could have looked at the universe all day. He imagined visiting them and discovering new animals and places. He had to pull himself away though, because the Gronad's wings were getting tired.

They flew back to the cave and Sam decided that he quite liked this ridiculous dragon. He spent a week with him, playing chess, exploring the caves in the mountains and generally having a good time. He eventually decided that he had better do his duty and find Honey and his horse and resume the commission he had to fulfil. *It's my duty as a Gillandite,* he thought, as he fumbled with the commission ring in his pocket.

'So then I came back here,' said Sam, finishing his tale to Ridge, Truss and Honey.

'So while we were all worried about you back here, you were enjoying yourself and having fun with that dragon,' said Honey. Sam detected a tone of jealousy in his voice.

'You weren't exactly waiting faithfully for Sam on the porch the whole time, Honey,' said Truss, smiling.

Honey coughed and pretended not to hear the comment. He went all quiet and sober for a while, and then said, 'So the Great Eagle kidnapped Tenga? And the Great Eagle tried to kill me. Sam, tell me who the bad guy is and who the good guy is – the Great Eagle, or Lord Mould?'

'Lord Mould is certainly against us and I don't know what the Great Eagle is up to, but as to who is evil and who is not, it's hard to tell. Oftentimes it is always the person that opposes you that is evil and your side is always good whoever you are, whether you're a Gillandite or a Clawlandite. Sometimes it is clear who the cruel one is. We shall have to wait until all the mysteries start to clear a bit. But it's no use,' said Sam, in a quiet voice. 'I didn't find Tenga at the Gronad's cave and Gilland is going to lose this battle.'

'Now you're talking some sense,' said Truss.

'How do you know Gilland's going to lose?' asked Ridge.

'When we were in that fog on the river, I saw in Lord Mould's eyes the city of Gilland burning and the Gillandites fleeing for their lives.'

'You say Tenga was taken to Clawland?' Honey got up from his chair. 'Then what in the world are we waiting for? Let's go find Tenga there!' Honey rushed to get packed.

'I'll come with you. We'll sail a ship along the sea and approach Clawland round the back,' said Truss. 'Oh, and by the way, I found your horse, Sam. I didn't want to tell anyone as I intended to keep him if you didn't come back.'

'Well, then I suppose that's decided,' said Sam with a gleam in his eyes again. 'We sail tomorrow morning!'

Chapter 13

All Paws on Deck!

Sam and Honey led their horse and donkey and all their provisions down to the docks. It was a fairly sunny morning with a gentle wind – a perfect day for sailing. Moored at the largest dock was a magnificent sailing ship with three masts. The ship was a majestic dark mahogany with golden patterns of birds and vines on its sides, and on the bow was a carving of a cat. The provisions and the horses were loaded on the ship by ropes and pulleys, and soon all was ready to depart. The crew got on first, followed by the captain, a wolf, and a graceful looking white cat.

'The ship belongs to her,' said Truss as they waited for the passengers to board.

Sam stared at the cat as she walked up the gangplank, elegantly twitching her tail with excitement. *What a lovely cat!* thought Sam.

He turned around to see what Honey was up to and almost wished he hadn't seen. Honey was signing his autograph for all of his many Endworlder fans, promising each one that he'll come back as soon as possible. They took a fond farewell of Ridge and boarded the ship. Sam noticed that Honey's eyes were wet as he waved goodbye to the Endworlders while the ship pulled away from the dock.

They sailed towards the west and Sam saw the valley that lead to the Gronad's cave in the distance. He smiled as he remembered the odd dragon, but turned his mind back to the ship.

Just then he saw the white cat walking along the deck. Her fur was nicely combed and her whiskers straightened. She wore rich garments and very expensive-looking jewels. And every so often she would check her reflection in the brass fittings of the ship. Sam strolled towards her and tried to look as if he hadn't noticed her, but he straightened his clothes a bit and smoothed down the fur on his head.

'Oh, hello,' he said carelessly to her. 'I hear that this ship belongs to you?'

'Of course. It is a rather beautiful ship isn't it?' She talked in a smooth, purring voice.

'What's your name?'

'Madeline, but most animals call me Maddy,' she purred.

'A Gillandite name.' Sam was keen to keep the conversation going.

'It *is* a rather beautiful name, isn't it?'

'Why, yes,' said Sam

'My parents were from Gilland, but I grew up as an Endworlder and I've never been to Gilland. Don't you think my fur looks nice today?' She was purring full time by this stage.

Sam rather liked the vain cat. 'You do look nice today,' he said putting on the nicest smile he could.

Maddy was so pleased that she almost choked from purring so loudly. Just then Honey came to see what was going on.

'Aw, aren't you two sweet,' he said with a patronising air. 'Why don't you just ask her to marry you and get it all over and done with?'

If Sam had been another colour from black, he would have turned bright red.

'Go away Honey, stop being so stupid!'

'I beg your pardon Sammy, but I am definitely *not* stupid. In fact you have not yet seen the full extent of my intelligence.' With that, Honey lectured Sam and Maddy for the next half hour on how clever he was.

All that evening Honey sat quietly on his bed in the cabin, scheming up a way to get Maddy and Sam to agree to get married without all the tidying of fur and being as pleasant as you can nonsense which, he thought, would just degrade Sam to such a low level of softness that he couldn't just stand by and watch it happen.

In such a time as this, when danger is hovering over him, my brains must help my little brother, thought Honey. Eventually he had a plan, which he would put into execution the following morning.

The morning was bright and summery and a cool breeze brushed lightly against Maddy's fur as she came out on deck for a walk. Honey was trying to hide himself behind one of the masts, but sneezed a few times and Maddy soon discovered he was there.

'I was just inspecting the mast,' said Honey. 'I'm

quite a professional when it comes to ships. In fact, I'm quite a professional when it comes to anything. Sam always needs my brains around.'

Maddy's whiskers and ears twitched forwards at the mention of Sam.

'But I'll tell you what the most interesting thing about this ship is, and that's the fact that the wheels are so well hidden that you can't see them.'

Honey took Maddy to the side of the ship. Maddy laughed, but decided to humour Honey a bit, so she looked over the edge into the water to pretend to look for the wheels. Honey started whistling loudly and then quickly shoved Maddy over the side of the ship, into the water.

'HELP! HELP!' he shouted in a voice exactly like when he used to act out things for his family when he and Sam were puppies. 'Cat overboard! Sam, HELP!'

Sam and a few others came rushing out to see what Honey was on about.

'I think this is a job for Sam,' said Honey. Then he looked into the water and was surprised to see that Maddy had disappeared. 'She was there a minute ago.'

Honey was very confused. Sam and Truss ran to the stern of the ship and saw Maddy frantically trying to stay above water, mewing piteously. Sam got a rope and tied it around him and told Truss to hold the other end. Without a moment's hesitation, he jumped into the water to save the poor cat. Honey was running around on deck with excitement; he was so pleased to see that his plan was working. Soon the soaking Maddy and Sam were back on the ship.

Maddy was furious.

'Just look at me now!' she hissed. 'My fur is all ruined and salty.'

'This is the time to propose to her Sam!' Honey announced in front of everyone.

'Go away Honey! I wish I had never taken you with me to look for Tenga, you just spoil everything!' Sam shouted.

Honey's tail tucked under and his bottom lip began to quiver. 'I was only trying to help.'

'Well, just stay out of everything next time,' Sam growled at Honey and told him to go back into the cabin.

But despite the fact that Maddy had almost drowned, the plan had actually worked. Maddy became very fond of Sam for saving her and it was hardly a few days until Sam told Maddy that he would come back to marry her once the battle against Lord Mould had finished, whether Gilland won or not.

Honey was so pleased with the outcome that he went around telling every single animal on the ship the story of how he had made up such a brilliant plan in saving his brother. And when everyone was obviously tired of Honey constantly talking about it, he composed a song to sing to the Endworlders once he got back there. Sam was still cross with his brother for a while but soon forgave him, and life went on as normal on the ship until the fifth day of the voyage.

Sam was sitting on the deck with Maddy, telling her all about how he had escaped from the Clawland prison, when he saw a dark creature swimming in the water. He got up and went to the bow of the ship. The creature came closer and stopped in front of the ship. As the ship neared it, he recognised it to be Lord Mould's pet. Suddenly it lifted its head and gave a loud cry, then dived into the water and disappeared.

The water grew dark as the skies filled with storm clouds, and Sam felt a spot of rain on his shoulder. Soon everyone was running around making ready for the storm. Eventually the storm hit with a flash of lighting and a strong gust of wind. Then the rain came down in sheets and the waves tossed the ship around like an angry child with a toy boat.

Maddy ran below deck with Honey, and Sam and Truss helped the others who were trying to bail out as much water as they could and throw all the heavy cargo into the sea. The captain shouted orders but they were lost in the sound of the raging storm. Soon the crew were in chaos and nobody quite knew what they were supposed to do.

Sam staggered up to the captain. 'Do you think you can weather this storm?' he shouted.

'I'm not sure I can hold this ship against it too much longer,' shouted back the captain. 'We may have to abandon ship.'

'Look!' said Sam, his eyes widening. 'Steer to the left, or we'll be thrown over the edge of the world!' but the captain could do nothing.

Sam ran down below deck and dragged Honey and Maddy out into the storm. He lowered one of the lifeboats and put them in, then ran to the hold to get Balaam and Strawberry. Once the horse and donkey were on the lifeboat, he cut the ropes and he and Truss jumped in.

'Try and row to shore!' he shouted to Truss. 'The ship is lost.'

Maddy was stunned with horror as she saw her lovely ship tip onto its side and disappear over the edge of the world. Sam thought of his ride on the

Gronad and wondered what the animals on the ship were experiencing now, if they were still alive. But they were not out of danger themselves; their tiny vessel was also being hurled towards the waterfall.

Then the storm suddenly lifted, as if its sole purpose was to get rid of the ship, and Sam and Truss had an easier time combating the raging sea. So eventually they managed to beach on the shore.

'Where do you suppose we are, Sammaramus?' said Honey, getting out of the boat.

'I don't know, but we better head east.' He looked at the mountains and saw a passage through them. 'I think it would be best if we went on the other side of the mountain range. This sea is not safe.'

Sam and Maddy mounted Strawberry, and Honey and Truss managed to ride the strong donkey. In such manner they entered the narrow valley, and were soon on the other side of the mountain range where they were in green pastureland and meadows.

'Now to Clawland,' said Sam.

He and the rest of the company began to ride towards Clawland with the mountain range on their right. It was a long road ahead of them and they had no provisions. They would have to find a village or a town somewhere to get food or else they would starve, because the sheep and cattle were far too wild to catch.

'We're bound to come across some settlement,' Sam said, but secretly he was worried.

'And no paper and pen to write songs or draw pictures!' Honey's ears drooped. 'What if I have a moment of inspiration? This could be a world disaster, if I can't produce my songs!'

Chapter 14

Friend or Foe?

Just as the little company were relaxing to a comfortable ride, Sam espied, out of the corner of his eye, Lord Mould's pet crawling down the side of a mountain just next to them. It had a torch of fire in its mouth and, as swift as the wind, it had them trapped in a circle of fire.

'Now I have you!' said the creature in a voice a little like Lord Mould's. 'You shall not find Tenga!

Your country will be destroyed and my master shall rule that seaport. He has told me to kill you, which I shall do with my whole heart.' It leaped into the circle of fire and bared its yellow teeth at Maddy.

Sam and Truss got out their swords and faced the creature. Maddy's fur was puffed out with fear, but she grabbed Honey's sword out of its sheath and brandished it in front of Lord Mould's pet. The creature grinned as it stepped away from Maddy and approached Sam.

'You're the one, black knight. You're the one that has the commission from King Farratol of Gilland.' It jumped on Sam and bit into his right arm. Sam's sword flew from his paw and he cried out in pain.

Truss ran to the creature with sword outstretched, ready to kill him with one powerful thrust. But Lord Mould's pet was too quick and, before the sword could touch the creature, Truss found his sword knocked out of his paw and he was faced by the grinning beast.

'What made you think that you could kill me?' It snarled at Truss and turned back to finish off Sam. Just as he was about to pounce on Sam, a voice echoed through the mountains.

'Leave them alone for now, they have the yellow

pup with them.'

'Yes, master.' The beast made one last threatening snap at the company of animals and slunk away. The fire around them died down and Truss began to try to quieten the horse and donkey, ready to move on.

Maddy rushed to where Sam sat panting on the ground. 'You're hurt Sam!'

'Just a little.' His right arm had a large gash in it. Maddy ripped off a strip of her cloak and wrapped it around the wound to stop it bleeding. Then she brought Sam's horse and helped him on.

'I can't fight now,' said Sam, as Maddy gave him his sword. 'That puts us in more risk of danger from that creature. We must be more wary in future.'

Maddy mounted the horse behind him and the animals rode on at a steady trot. Truss kept his sword drawn ready in case of an attack, much to the discomfort of Honey, who was afraid that he might poke his eye out by accident.

'What a pity I don't have a pen and paper with me,' said Honey, with a long drawn-out sigh. 'I would have liked to have written a song about that little encounter. Oh well, I suppose I shall just have to sing it a few times to remember it.'

Oh no! thought Sam, *not another one of his songs. I've*

just about had enough of them!

Honey cleared his throat and then began in an unrecognisable note,

'There once were four animals going for a ride,
And Lord Mould was not on their side
And when his pet attacked we wanted to hide
But if we did we might have died.

'Sam is hurt
But I'm not surprised,
'Cause he's stupid
He hasn't got brains like mine.'

Sam interrupted him. 'Honey, that last verse didn't even rhyme!'

'Haven't you ever heard of blank verse?' Honey replied. 'Sam I know you are stupid, but sometimes you astonish me with your astounding lack of knowledge.' Honey sang on at the top of his voice, and Sam felt genuine pity for the poor fox who sat behind the awful racket.

Eventually night fell and they tethered the horse and donkey to the ground to rest. Then they tried to get some sleep in a shallow cave in the side of a mountain.

Sam tossed and turned and wrapped his blanket

tight around him. He was shivering from a strange feeling of icy coldness. An hour or so later his blanket and cloak were folded up beside him as he was beginning to pant from heat. The wound in his arm stung as he dropped into a kind of waking dream.

He saw his father run past in front of him and he got up to follow the phantom. Sam staggered and stumbled as he followed his father, but managed to keep a few steps behind, although it still looked as if his father was running. He seemed to be following Rocky for ages, on and on, until the ground in front of them seemed to turn into marble, and Sam's father stopped in front of the throne in the palace of Gilland.

His father smiled at him. Sam stretched out his paw to touch him but he seemed just to grasp thin air. Rocky, his father, sat slowly down on the throne and Truss came into the throne room with the royal crown. As he placed it on Rocky's head, Sam's father began to slowly grow mouldy and deformed, his smile turned into the grin like the one on the face of Lord Mould's pet. Sam drew out his sword and slashed angrily at the air with it, and the phantoms disappeared.

His legs buckled under him and he found himself lying feverishly on the muddy river bank.

His arm ached and his head felt clouded. For a second his mind cleared and he knew he had a delirious fever.

'Get up!' Maddy was shaking Truss and Honey awake. 'Sam's gone. I woke up this morning and looked everywhere but I couldn't find him.' Maddy's whiskers were forward and tense.

The three searched around the place but could find no sign of Sam anywhere.

Truss sat down on a rock to think. 'Perhaps he was thirsty and went to the river to get a drink? Something may have happened to him there.'

Honey thought of the mist and the bridge, and shuddered at the thought of what might have happened to Sam.

'But the river's miles from here,' said Maddy. 'He can't have walked all the way there in the pitch dark – he would have at least have taken his horse.'

'We can but try,' said Truss as he jumped onto Sam's horse. 'It's either that or he's gone into the mountains.' He looked at the dangerous cliff faces and unstable ledges of the mountains. 'And there's little chance of survival if he went up there in the dark.'

They rode towards the river, keeping a lookout for any trace of the missing knight. After a long tedious ride they got to the riverbank, but there was still no sign of Sam.

'Honey, you take Balaam and Maddy and look for him along the river that way,' said Truss, pointing to the left, 'and I'll look for him downstream. We'll meet back here in an hour.' He cantered off along the river.

Honey and Maddy rode merely a few paces upstream when they glimpsed a black shape half submerged in water.

'That's Sam!' cried Honey. They called out for Truss who came back at a gallop. Then all three led the horse and donkey to where Sam was lying. Sam was muddied and wet from dew; he hardly responded as Honey and Truss dragged him onto the grass.

'Sammy, m'boy, are you alright?' Honey asked.

'My sword is mouldy,' Sam muttered.

'He's delirious,' said Truss undoing his bandage. His expression froze as he saw that the wound was ugly with a festering infection. 'We have to get him to a doctor quickly!' then, more to himself, 'Lord Mould will pay for this!'

They lifted Sam onto his horse and Truss mounted behind him. They galloped along the river hoping to come across a village or town. After a while the river widened rapidly until it was very wide indeed, looking more like a lake than a river.

Spanning this wide section of the river were bridges and huts. They galloped to a bridge that branched off in different directions, much like streets and lanes. The bridges were crowded with animals of all sorts, who stared at the riders as their mounts' hooves made a thumping sound on the wooden boards of the bridge.

'We need a doctor,' said Truss to an idle squirrel, which just stared back at him. 'We need a doctor now!' Truss began to get angry.

Then a hare came forward and asked, 'Who are you?'

'We are travellers from Gilland, on a commission from the King.' Truss brought out the commission ring from Sam's pocket. 'Bring us to the ruler of this town.'

'I am the mayor,' said the Hare quietly. 'Come to my hut, I have a doctor there.'

They followed the Hare to a very large hut, tied the horse and donkey to the railing outside and walked up the steps into the Hare's home.

'You may put your friend in that room there and my private doctor shall be through to see him.' The Hare pointed to a door on his left and Truss helped Sam in and laid him on a large bed. Maddy stayed with Sam while Truss and Honey followed the Hare through to the living room.

'What's your business here?' The Hare's voice was quiet and calm. He was dressed in sheepskin clothes and his long ears were jet black, as were his beady eyes.

'We are on our way to Clawland in preparation for the battle between our countries. On the way we were attacked by Lord Mould's pet and our friend, Sam, was bitten. Then the wound got badly infected so we had to find some help.' Truss licked his lips nervously.

Honey didn't like the tension in the room so decided to heroically make things a little more light-hearted.

'Yeah, and I made up a song about it. It's really good; the others listened to it for hours and were so overcome by it that they had to shut their ears. I'm sure you would like me to sing it to you!' Honey smiled and wagged his tail, he was sure that his talent would be appreciated here as it was at the Endworlder village.

The Hare scowled at him. 'I have no need of your singing.'

Honey's tail stopped wagging. 'Well, I think you are a stuck up, stupid rabbit!'

'Be quiet, Honey, before you get us into big

trouble,' Truss whispered.

The Hare turned his attention back to Truss. 'You don't have a Gillandite accent, it is more like that of Clawland.'

'I was a Clawlandite but decided to join the Gillandites' side.' Truss's eyes searched the room and the Hare's face for any clues as to their loyalties.

'A traitor!' the Hare's beady eyes flashed with anger. 'Unfortunately for you, we are in alliance with the Clawlandites. Once your friend is better we will hand you over to the mercy of Lord Mould!' He called for a servant. 'Lock these fellows and the cat in the dungeon.'

The servant, a squirrel, called some other animals and they took the weapons and armour from Honey and Truss, then brought Maddy through. They chained them and led them back across the bridge to the south bank and threw them in an iron-lined dungeon cut in the side of the riverbank. They closed the door.

Honey looked out of the bars at the water and the town.

'I have a feeling that we messed up a bit here,' he said.

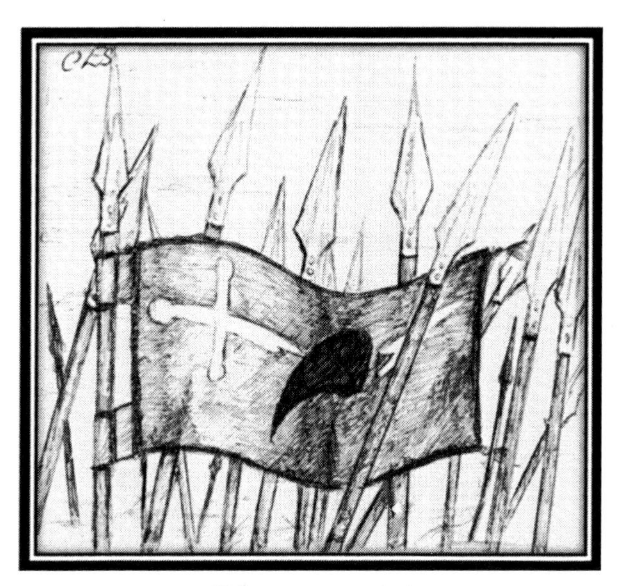

Chapter 15

To Clawland

Sam felt as if he was slowly coming out of a hazy fog. His arm was still rather painful but his mind was cleared and he could assess what was going on. The doctor told him where he was and informed him that his friends were in a dungeon waiting for him to get better, when they would then be taken to Lord Mould. The doctor, a tiger, seemed sympathetic to him and his friends.

'I think I might be able to help you,' said the doctor. 'I'll just say you're still too ill to go anywhere, which will give you time tonight to try and find the key to the dungeon. Then you and your friends can carry on with your journey. I worked in Gilland for a few years and liked it very much, so I'm keen to help.'

'You're so kind,' said Sam. 'Now tell me who has the keys and where I can find my friends' armour and swords.'

The doctor told Sam everything, including where Strawberry and Balaam were to be found in the stables. All was set for nightfall and a plan of action was thought out.

That night the doctor gave Sam his sword and armour. Then Sam crept quietly into the passage and opened the door of the Hare's bedroom. He quietly stepped in. He could hear heavy breathing: the Hare was still asleep.

He walked slowly to the chest of drawers. A floorboard creaked loudly as he put his weight on it. He froze as the Hare rolled onto his side, then all was still again. He gently opened the top drawer and saw the set of keys. He quickly grasped it with his paw and held it tight so that the keys would not clink together, then he carefully closed the drawer and crept back out into the passage.

Now I have the keys, thought Sam. *Where is the cellar?* He tried to remember the doctor's directions. *Ah, here it is!*

He unlocked a tiny door on the right and bent down to get through. It was dark inside but he could just make out an unlit torch on the wall. He closed the cellar door behind him and lit the torch with his tinderbox. The rays revealed a narrow winding staircase, cut out of a tree log, which led down into the darkness. *This must lead under the river!* He went cautiously down, and eventually reached the bottom. It was a large damp store room lined with iron to keep the water out. *Where on earth did they get all this iron from?* thought Sam. He rummaged around all the stores – barrels of wine, piles of sheepskin and leather, sacks of apples and wheat and all manner of foods for the winter. Sam took an apple and bit into it. He hadn't had an apple in such a long time!

Still eating, he rummaged around a bit more and finally found Honey and Truss' armour and weaponry. He picked it all up and threw his apple core into the corner of the cellar, and then made his way back up the winding stairs. When he got to the top he heard voices in the passageway on the other side if the door.

'The fool stole my keys!' the Hare was saying in

a sleepy voice.

'I'm sure you just misplaced them.' It was the doctor's voice.

Sam began to feel hot and a little shaky. The mayor was sure to guess that he was in the cellar and there was no way of getting past him without being seen. He put out the torch and waited in the dark to see what would happen. The doctor managed to draw the Hare away from the corridor, giving Sam a free passage for a few seconds. He opened the cellar door and ran to the front door, but he tripped and crashed heavily on the floor.

'There he is!' cried the squirrel servant, and he and some others started running towards Sam.

Sam jumped to his feet and ran out the front door. He rushed to the stables with them chasing close behind. He cut Strawberry and Balaam free and rode his horse bareback and led the donkey. He cantered along a bridge but pulled his horse to a sharp stop. The bridge suddenly ended and below him was the fast running water of the river. His pursuers were right behind him, so he had no choice. His horse reared as he tried to spur it on into the water. Just as he thought the whole plan had failed, Strawberry caught on to what was required of him and leapt into the river, followed by Honey's donkey. They swam as quickly as they could against the current to the dungeon in the side of the bank.

'Balaam!' cried Honey through the bars. 'My dear noble war horse. I've missed you so much!'

Sam raised his eyebrows and smiled. 'What about me, Honey, aren't you pleased to see me?' Sam unlocked the dungeon and they quickly climbed back onto the grasslands on the south side of the river.

'Sure I'm pleased to see you, Sam. But it's more the fact that you should be pleased to see me, because, after all, you can't really cope without my brains!'

Honey got onto his donkey with the help of Truss, as he found it difficult to mount without any stirrups.

'But you *would* have to leave the horses' saddles and reins, wouldn't you, Sam. Really, if only you had my intelligence!' Truss mounted behind Honey, and Sam helped Maddy onto the back of Strawberry.

'We must be quick!' said Sam, kicking his horse into a gallop. 'They'll be after us as soon as they tack up their horses.'

Indeed by the time dawn came their pursuers were gaining on them and they were soon galloping right behind Balaam, demanding Honey to stop. Truss drew out his sword as they came alongside them. It clashed with the enemy's sword and they were soon locked in a vicious duel. Honey was terrified, not so much of the enemy's sword, but more of Truss' sword which was being swung far too near his head for his liking. Eventually, though, Truss cut down the pursuers and jumped onto one of their horses, then they cantered along at a steady pace.

'If I hadn't ducked once or twice, I would have lost my head,' Honey was arguing with Truss. 'And then how do you suppose I'd be able to use my excellent brain? It will be gone, all because you can't control your weapon while riding!'

'I was in perfect control of what I was doing,' Truss answered.

'Stop arguing.' Sam slowed down his horse's pace to come alongside Balaam. 'It really doesn't matter!'

'Well, if you expect me to let this amateur ride with me at any stage again in the future, you have another think coming.' But just as he was complaining about Truss, he lost his balance and found himself rolling on the floor.

Sam and Truss laughed. 'And you think I'm the amateur one? You can't even ride a horse without stirrups!' Truss dismounted to help Honey back on the donkey.

'I didn't find that comment very funny!' Honey had turned a reddish colour with fury and embarrassment.

'Look!' said Maddy. She was pointing towards the mountains. 'We'd better hurry and find Tenga before it's too late.'

In the distance they saw a vast army, heavily armed, some on foot, some on horseback, and two divisions on huge elephants. The riders at the front held flags and were blowing eerie-sounding trumpets. The flags had a picture of a claw ripping a sword in two.

'The Clawlandite army,' said Truss, 'marching to the battlefield. It's over Sam.' They stared at the seemingly endless columns of Lord Mould's army.

Sam's horse grew impatient. It sensed battle and tossed its head with excitement.

'Not yet, all is not lost just yet,' said Sam, trying to keep his horse still. 'We must make all haste to Clawland and fulfil the commission before the battle starts.'

'They will be at the battlefield in about three days, and will be ready for battle on the fourth. We'll never do it in time!' said Truss. He got back on his horse. 'But you're the one with the commission, so we shall do as you say. My advice, however, is to go back to Gilland and help fight the war. You're a commander in the Black Knights Division One, Sam, they'll need you!'

Sam turned his horse to the east. 'We go to find Tenga in Clawland.' Then he turned around to Truss again. 'But it's not safe for Maddy. She must go back to her Endworld village. You must take her, Truss.'

'I think you're right.' Truss got down from his horse and helped Maddy off Strawberry and onto his own horse. 'Oh Sam, you'll need these.' Truss tossed Sam some Clawlandite garments. 'And try to copy my accent as best you can.'

'Thanks Truss,' said Sam. Then he turned to Maddy. 'When we've finished with this battle, I'll fulfil my promise, Maddy. Remember that.' Sam kissed Maddy's paw, then the two parties separated. Honey and Sam cantered towards Clawland, and Maddy and Truss trotted off to the end of the world.

'Nice cat, isn't she?' Honey had become very bored after riding for a while. 'I think I'll make a song about you and her – *The Knight and the Pussy Cat.*'

'Fine. But it might be best if you keep it in your head rather than sing it now; then you can surprise us and sing it on our wedding day.' Sam was sure

Honey would forget about it by then.

'Good idea.' Honey was quiet for a while, then said, 'Sammy, I'm so hungry, I haven't eaten since we were in that cosy prison cell.'

'Well, you'll just have to wait until we get to Clawland.'

'When will we get there?' Honey half hoped that Sam would say that they were just about there now.

'Probably by sundown.'

'Sundown!' Honey suddenly pulled his donkey to a walk and stared at Sam as the solemn fact sunk in. 'I'm sure I'll die of starvation before then!'

'I doubt it.' Sam was not in the mood for talking. His thoughts were with a white cat a few miles away from them.

Honey realised this and heroically decided to talk to Balaam instead. He chatted quite happily about this and that, and about how stupid his brother was and how clever he was. It seemed like only a few minutes before they entered the wastelands that surrounded Clawland, and the sun began to creep and hide behind the mountains. They stopped and dismounted at a slight rise in the ground, where they could see the city of Clawland stretched before them, dark and forbidding.

Chapter 16

A Dead City and a Dead Hope

Sam and Honey found a good spot to change into their Clawlandite disguise, after which Sam put their Gillandite armour and swords into a sack and tied it to Balaam. When all this preparation was completed the two dogs proceeded to the gates of the city.

'What happens if we don't find Tenga here, Sammy?' asked Honey.

'Gilland is lost and the world will rot with the filth of Lord Mould.'

Honey gulped, 'But he is here, isn't he?'

'He's bound to be.' Sam turned his attention to the gatekeeper. He tried to speak as much like Truss as possible. 'We are citizens here, come back from a long journey.'

The gatekeeper grunted and opened the gates. Sam and Honey entered to find the city damp and filthy. The narrow streets and tall houses blocked out the sunset and cast shadows on all inside the city gates. The inhabitants seemed given up to drunkenness and laziness.

'No wonder we're fighting for Gilland!' whispered Honey to Sam.

'Honey, please do as little talking as possible.'

They rounded a bend and came to a narrow street, at the end of which was an inn with a gnarled olive tree in the middle of the courtyard.

'We shall stay here for the night and get food and water.' Sam gave the horse and donkey to the stable kitten, and took the sack with them into the inn. The inside of the boarding lodge was crowded with scruffy-looking animals, loud and rowdy.

'We need a room for the night,' said Sam to the inn keeper. The inn keeper looked at Sam for a long time. *He's probably detected my accent!* thought

Sam. But the inn keeper gave them the key to their room, and a candle and directions, and said nothing else.

They went up three flights of stairs and along the landing to the left, into a small dirty room. The ceiling was low and Honey immediately knocked his head and cried out.

'You must keep quiet,' said Sam. 'Anyone can pick out your accent!'

Sam looked out of the small window. He could see the city looking old and tired. He could well imagine what it must have been like in its prime, before Lord Mould corrupted it. He saw Lord Mould's castle towering above the city, and he shuddered at the thought that they would have to go there tomorrow. Directly below the castle he recognised the prison that they had been kept in, all those months ago. Just then, someone knocked on the door. Sam went to open it.

'The food you ordered.' It was the inn keeper.

'Thank you.' Sam took the food and closed the door. It tasted strange and not to Sam's liking, but he was very hungry, so ate it heartily.

'This is good stuff, Sam!' Honey was wolfing down his food. 'You don't get this quality in Gilland.'

'Actually, I don't like it very much.'

Honey stared at Sam for a bit. 'I always knew you were mad, m'boy.' Honey shook his head slowly. 'You're a sad case.'

'We better get some sleep.' Sam finished his dinner and jumped onto the bed nearest the window. 'Tomorrow we go to the castle, and there our fate will be decided.' He pulled the blankets up to his chin and quickly fell into a troubled dream.

***

The next morning was grey and wet as Sam and Honey rode away from the inn. They passed the olive tree in the courtyard and Honey was delighted to see a rough-looking rabbit sound asleep in one of the branches.

'Notice that, Sam,' said Honey. 'A rabbit living in a tree, just as I told you they did.'

Sam smiled.

Just at that minute the rabbit fell out of the tree and woke up. 'Oh, and look Sam,' said Honey, wagging his tail, 'just the way I told you!'

'Just because you see one rabbit sleeping in a tree doesn't mean that living in trees is a rabbit's natural habitat,' said Sam.

Honey was so confused by what Sam had just said. *'Natural habitat'? What in the world is that supposed to mean?* he thought, but decided to carry on with the humiliating of Sam.

'You see, Sam, you always think you're right and think you can prove it; but really, I'm the one that's always right and that has already been proven.'

'Never mind. What's important now is to find Tenga quickly. We can't dawdle here all day.'

Sam kicked his horse into a trot and they rode along the main street. The street was on a slight incline and very crowded. To make things harder, the cobbles were wet and slippery, so the horse and donkey had no choice but to proceed at a slow walk.

Despite Sam's frustration, he was intrigued by all the goings on in the city. Cubs and puppies and kittens and all kinds of young animals played happily in the crowded streets, playing hide and seek among the vast sea of animals. Sam noticed that the young animals had no back gardens or greens to play in like in Gilland, as the whole city seemed to be all stone and cobbles.

The female animals went about their domestic business, buying food from the traders that had set up their stalls on the side of the street, scolding the little ones for getting so muddy and wet, and hanging their washing out on the washing lines that stretched from one side of the street to the other. These washing lines were all along the street and blocked out what little light was able to creep its way through the clouds and squeeze itself into the narrow streets and lanes of the city.

Many of the adult male animals were absent. *Probably conscripted into the army,* thought Sam. Those that were left were very old, or very young. In each face Sam studied, he only saw normal animals, like in his own country, wishing for comfort and peace. *Can these be our enemies?*

There were grand buildings scattered here and there – theatres, banqueting halls, colleges. All had impressive engravings of stone on them, crumbled and eroded – the ghosts of better days long forgotten.

'Ain't this such a fun-looking place to live!' Honey seemed delighted by the scruffiness and untidiness of Clawland.

'No,' said Sam quietly to himself, 'it feels like a sad town, ashamed of what it has become, wishing to return to its former splendour. You can see it in all the animals' faces.'

They soon left the crowded streets and Sam left his ponderings with them. His thoughts turned to more tangible matters as they approached the drawbridge of the dark castle. They trotted across the drawbridge and up to the guards of the castle.

'What's your business?' said a sour-looking guard.

'We need to see Lord Mould on important business regarding the war,' said Sam in his best Clawlandite accent.

'Lord Mould is marching to the battlefields near Gilland right now. He will be back in a few weeks' time.'

'We must be allowed in!' Sam hadn't thought of the problem of getting into the castle. Sam looked at the two guards. *So little security!* thought Sam. As quick as lightning he grabbed his sword from the sack and cut down the guards.

'Quick, Honey, before someone else comes!'

Sam and Honey cantered into the courtyard of the castle and quickly put Strawberry and Balaam into the stables. Then they ran through a door next to the stables. Everything was quiet as the two dogs stepped into the corridor, at the end of which was a large hall. There was no sign of life anywhere. Thin streams of light came from windows cut high into the wall revealing a long, empty table. The wood was rotten and eaten by woodworms. A thick layer of dust lay on it. On the walls around the room were paintings, all faded and covered in dust and mould. This was nothing like Sam had expected.

'We must split up and search the place for any sign of Tenga. I'll take this door on the right, and you take that door, then we'll meet back down here.'

Sam opened a door on the right which lead to a winding staircase. *This must be one of the towers,* thought Sam. He ran up the stairs until he got to a ladder which took him into a small empty room. He was annoyed and ran back down. He explored a number of rooms and halls but all had the same theme – dust, faded pictures and carpets, moth-eaten furniture and curtains, mould and worm-eaten wood.

Everywhere he went it was as quiet as death with no sign of a living creature anywhere. Eventually he came to another tower. At the top he froze with amazement. The small window let in a golden ray of light that lit up the tiny room. The floor of the room was covered with old decaying toys, and in the corner he noticed a cot and a little rocking horse. *What can all this mean?* Sam's mind was thick with many thoughts, all crowding into his head at once, but he couldn't work out this place. He climbed slowly down the winding stairs of the tower and met Honey, who was waiting for him back in the hall.

'Find anything, Honey?' asked Sam.

'No.' Honey seemed strangely solemn and quiet.

Sam sighed. 'We've failed, Honey. We didn't find Tenga. Lord Mould will wage war and capture Gilland, thus becoming ruler of the east and west. Eventually he will battle against the south Endworlders and become mighty enough to defeat the Great Eagle and capture the north. Very soon, Lord Mould and his filth and greed shall rule the world, all because I was not diligent enough to find Tenga.'

Sam didn't feel like going anywhere. This place seemed so quiet and dead and the fact that he couldn't fulfil the commission sunk painfully in.

He leaned against the wall. *Why must it end like this? Why must the world be covered in darkness without one single glimmer of hope?*

He wandered around the hall trying to figure out what the faded paintings were, and just tried not to think. Some of the bigger pictures he recognised as battles and scenes of feasts and merry making – paintings of victory. The faded figures seemed like images of ghosts. They seemed to point a paw, or a wing, or a claw at him saying, 'You failed!' The rotten banqueting table in the middle of the hall seemed to mock him saying, 'Many noble animals sat around me after they had come back from victory, but you failed!' The hopeful rays of light streaming through the window seemed a mere mockery.

He reached into his pocket and brought out the commission ring. He had been so proud to receive it, but oh how he hated it now! He threw it across the hall, but from there it stared accusingly back at him. He tried to bury it in the blankets inside the sack, but from there it still gnawed on his mind, constantly accusing him. 'You failed!'

Chapter 17

Coming Home

Sam and Honey walked away from the castle. Sam led his horse; he didn't feel like riding it. It was large and he would be sticking out proudly from the crowd. On the way to the castle he had enjoyed the sense of superiority, but now he wanted to get lost in the crowd. He felt as if everyone could look straight through him and see his shame.

He looked at the animals he passed in a different light, he understood them now. He understood the feeling of a lost hope and the crumbling of everything that meant anything to him. Neither he nor Honey spoke, but both walked aimlessly around the city in silence. Sam didn't care where they were going and they were soon lost. They turned into a back lane and were faced by two animals dressed in hooded cloaks.

'Are you Sam? The one with the commission from the king of Gilland?' said one of them.

Every muscle in Sam's body began to tense. *Who are these animals?* But he recognised the Gillandite accent, so replied, 'I am indeed.'

'Come with us quickly!' They hurried him and Honey into a run-down house.

'Who are you?' said Sam with his sword drawn.

The animals took their cloaks off and revealed themselves. One was a bear and the other a weasel. Sam immediately recognised them as Farratol's messengers.

'We've come straight from the King. Lord Mould's army are encamped at the battlefield and the battle will begin tomorrow. The King has sent me to tell you that he requires your presence at once,' said the weasel in a thin, sharp voice.

'But we can't get there in time!' said Sam. 'It's a

four days' gallop from here.'

'A friend of yours has offered to take you there,' said the bear with a slight smile.

'A friend of ours?' Sam couldn't think who the messenger was talking about.

'You'll see. He's waiting for us in the scorched field just outside the gate,' said the bear. 'Now go quickly and get your Gillandite armour and cloaks on, and we'll be off.'

Accordingly, Honey and Sam changed back into the uncomfortable armour, and then joined the messengers outside.

'You lost your horse's saddle and armour?' asked the weasel.

'Yes, but at least I was trained to ride bareback when I was a squire, not like certain soldiers who belong in the Rook Division!' Sam smiled at Honey.

They were both in a better mood, although Sam was worried about what he would say to the King. They rode out through the gates and there, trying to hide behind some dead bushes, was the Gronad! Honey immediately started galloping the other way, shouting that they were all going to be eaten, but Sam managed to calm him down.

'He's actually my friend, Honey,' said Sam. 'Don't you remember me telling you?'

'All I can say, Sam, is that you are absolutely mad, weird and stupid. You, a knight, making friends with a dragon!' Honey shook his head. 'You are hopeless, Sam.'

Just then the Gronad noticed Sam and crawled towards him.

'So nice to eat – I mean, *meet* you again!' The huge dragon's tail swayed back and forth with excitement. 'Get on my back, both of you. I agreed to take you to Gilland.'

Sam and Honey climbed onto the Gronad's back, and the Gronad picked up the terrified donkey and horse with its front legs, and leaped into the air.

As they flew far away from Clawland, Sam had a thought.

'Seeing as you're going to be in the Gilland area, why don't you help us fight?'

The Gronad tossed up its small head and its ears pricked up.

'Me, fight? Why, that's absurd! I'm scared stiff of battles. Wouldn't be in one for anything.' It shook its head.

Honey decided at that moment that he really liked the Gronad.

'I agree with you totally. It is a stupid thing to be in a battle and it's a lot better to stay away from danger,' and for the next hour or so Honey and the Gronad chatted on together about how clever it was to stay away from anything harmful, and how stupid Sam was to like wars.

I knew Honey would be able to identify with this creature! thought Sam. But that wasn't the worst. Eventually Honey and the Gronad began to sing each other songs they had made up, and then they decided to make a song together. The first verse went something like this:

'Oh how nice it is to be flying,
Not just sitting in a cave and frying
From the heat that is too hot for a dog
But not for a dragon who looks like a frog.'

Sam sighed. 'It's bad enough having just one singing, but two is unbearable!'

'Just ignore my little brother,' said Honey. 'He suffers from a severe case of madness and doesn't appreciate talent.' The Gronad nodded in agreement.

Soon the conversation turned to Honey lecturing the Gronad on how astonishingly clever he was; and the Gronad informing Honey, in great detail, on how clever *he* was. Sam was relieved to see them dropping down through the clouds just above Gilland, else he was sure that the pleasant conversation would turn into a hot argument, the air being already hot enough from the Gronad's breathing.

They alighted next to the fountain in the huge courtyard of the palace, while all the animals stared at them from safe distances. Sam got off and tried to look as if it was the most normal thing in the world to ride a dragon, but inside he was enjoying seeing everyone's amazement.

When they had dismounted, the Gronad gave them a tearful farewell, which embarrassed Sam immensely, and then it flew off, back to its lonely cave. A young puppy came and took Balaam and Strawberry to the stables, and Sam and Honey went into the palace. The clean walls and floors and the riches evident around the palace as they walked to the throne room made such a nice change from the sad forsaken castle of Clawland.

King Farratol was sitting stone-still at the chess board, and did not respond to Sam and Honey's entrance.

'Your Majesty,' said Sam, licking his lips with nervousness, 'you called for us.'

The King slowly turned around and said, 'Yes I did.' His eyes looked from Sam to Honey and then back to Sam again. It was clear to Sam that he was expecting them to have brought Tenga.

Sam took in a deep breath and said, quite simply, 'We looked everywhere, but couldn't find him.' Sam expected the King to show some emotion, but the King was calm and quiet. 'Lord Mould took him,' Sam continued, 'but we have no idea what happened to him.'

'This is the end then.' The King sat heavily on his throne. 'This day will be the last day of freedom and peace. Let's make the most of it.' The King got up with a determined expression on his face. 'You will join me in a feast tonight?'

'Certainly!' said Honey, wagging his tail and licking his lips. 'I can sing you one of my many songs that I made up on our journey!'

The King smiled at Honey, then his face grew serious again and he turned to Sam. 'We will meet our end as a true Gillandite should – with valour and honour and love to our country!'

Sam took a step back and bowed. Honey also tried to bow, but failed and ended up on the polished floor, rubbing his sore nose.

The banquet that night was pleasant and Sam recounted their adventures to the nobles and lords, while Honey sang and drank with the soldiers and common animals. They did not appreciate his 'talent' quite as much as the Endworlders, but he had a fun time nonetheless.

During the banquet, the King took Sam to the throne room and showed him the chess game.

'The only slight hope for us, Sam, is for you to duel with Lord Mould.'

Sam stared at the King. 'But only his bloodline can kill him!'

The King nodded slowly. 'We have no real hope, Sam, but this will show the enemy that we will not die easily, but will fight to the bitter end.'

Sam looked solemnly at the black knight piece in the corner of the board, then he looked the King straight in the eyes. 'For valour and for Gilland?'

'For valour and for Gilland,' the King replied.

'Then that's decided.' Sam and the King went back to the banqueting hall and tried to look as confident as possible; the Gillandites' moral must be kept up.

After the feast Sam went back to Honey's house. It was just how they had left it, as if it had been waiting patiently for their return. Even the book with the description of the Gronad still lay open on the table.

Sam wandered around the house that held so many memories. It was the place they had grown up. Sam smiled as he came to the loose stair that had never been fixed. He and Honey had kept in there a secret stash of food and other things they had collected. He wandered upstairs to the little bedroom they had shared. The springs in the beds were broken from when they had pillow-fights and played at knights and dragons. He looked out of the window and saw the gnarled old tree they used to play in, and remembered the time when he had pushed Honey out while playing 'Dog Overboard!' Honey had broken his leg, so they were banned from playing that game.

He brushed his paw along the books that Sam had read to Honey each night. He came across a book that he hadn't noticed before and called Honey up to ask where he got it from.

'Oh, that was Tenga's. He left it here when he was playing with Owl,' said Honey. 'I put it there for his return.'

Sam remembered the little cub as he was, and realised that that was what he was searching for – not the fulfilment of an agreement to save Gilland, but a search to find a little fun-loving cub, and in him rediscover his own childhood long past.

Chapter 18

The Final Battle

In the morning, Sam and Honey had a hearty breakfast, full of joking and laughing. Sam was even happy to have Honey show him his collection of pictures, after which Sam got up from the table and went to get ready for battle. He was soon mounted on his horse, ready to go to the meeting of the cavalry. He said goodbye to Honey and promised to meet him by the fountain in the courtyard of the palace for one last time before the fighting began.

The cavalry meeting consisted of a lion, the baron of the two divisions of knights, briefing the two commanding officers of the battle plans. The plans were grim and hopeless, but Sam could not help a feeling of immense excitement creep into him. He was a knight after all, and the battlefield was a place of excitement and honour. A Gillandite knight was not to regard it as a place of death, but rather a place of victory, even if the battle went ill.

'This battle is going to be like none other, there will be no cavalry charges' the baron was saying. 'Today we have to fight as if we were in a chess game, so each move we do has been decided and planned beforehand. Our whole trust lies in the King now. The moves he makes on a little chessboard determine the fate of us each.' He pointed at one of the black knights on a chessboard. 'This black knight is you, Sam, and all the other five knights in your division.'

He went through all the moves carefully with Sam, and Sam recorded them in his memory. Finally, the baron came to the last move.

'By the time you get to this space to fight Lord Mould, you will most likely be on your own.' He pointed to a black square at the top left corner of the board. In the square directly to the right of it, in the corner square, was the white King – Lord Mould. 'Lord Mould will then duel with you and undoubtedly kill you.' He calmly moved the white king to take the black knight. 'After you have been taken, the Gillandite Queen Division will move to the far end of the chess board and checkmate the white king.'

Sam's eyes grew wide. 'Then that means Gilland has won!'

'No.' The baron frowned. 'There was one part of the chess game that Lord Mould kept in high secrecy. Even the Clawlandite fox could not find that bit out. The likelihood is that our Queen Division will be taken before that stage. All King Farratol could do was weigh probabilities, and this is our only chance. Lord Mould is a cunning fellow.'

Sam sighed as he looked at the fallen knight chess piece. 'Our lives decided by a game used for pleasure! What has the world come to?'

The cavalry meeting was soon over and Sam met Honey at the fountain as arranged.

'Oh Sammy, m'boy, you'll never guess what!' Honey had just been at the Rook meeting, and he was excited and nervous. 'The Rook Divisions are going to be riding...elephants!' Honey nearly jumped up and down with pleasure, but just managed to control himself.

'Did they teach you how to manage those animals when you were training?' Sam looked doubtful, but was pleased to see Honey was looking forward to the battle.

'Oh yes, we just never expected that we would ever get to do it.' But before they could say more, the trumpet sounded for the army to group. Sam said a hasty farewell to his brother and rushed to the cavalry's stable.

Twelve horses were ready with their armour on; twelve horses pawing impatiently at the ground for the battle to begin; twelve horses about to lead their riders to a glorious death, and the twelve knights were as keen as they.

Sam stroked Strawberry's chin.

'Today is the day of days, Strawberry. Today you must show the Clawlandites what speed and agility means.' He mounted his noble black horse and cantered into the stable yard. He shouted encouragement to his five fellow knights, and then the two divisions trotted to the battlefield.

The commanding officer of the other Black Knight Division trotted next to Sam.

'Today is a day for the Gillandite Knights!' he

said, then cantered off with his five knights to the left side of the battlefield.

Sam took his knights to the right side and they stopped in a row with the Rook Division on their right and the Bishop Division on their left. Sam saw Honey laughing and messing around with his fellow Rooks on a huge elephant. The Rook Division had always been an unruly lot. There were a total of ten elephants in the Gillandite army and the other divisions were also large.

A great army! thought Sam, but his thoughts clouded slightly as he saw the magnificence of the Clawlandite army grouping on the opposite side of the battlefield.

Then King Farratol came, riding a black and white horse with heavy armour. He cantered past the normal soldiers stretched out in the front, and headed toward the middle of the battlefield, where he pulled his horse to a sharp stop and waited. Eventually a dark figure cantered up to meet King Farratol and stopped in front of him. It was Lord Mould. Sam knew that the Kings were exchanging speeches, as is the usual custom before battles. After that, the King came galloping back. He halted at the Gillandite lines and blew a ram's horn trumpet. The battle had begun!

Sam was keen to start fighting, but kept still as

he watched the different sides taking turns moving their divisions. It was so exactly like a giant chess game that Sam was amazed. The only thing different was that moving onto a 'square' in pursuit of the other army didn't mean that you had taken the enemy. After a few moves on either side, two opposing divisions of common soldiers met and the fighting began.

The Clawlandite division killed the Gillandite division. *Such an absurd battle!* thought Sam. He was growing restless and could hardly keep his horse still. Soon almost all the divisions of the armies were locked in combat and it looked more like a proper battle.

The air was thick with arrows as Sam and his Division made their first move. *About two hundred horse's strides from the right side, and two hundred from the back of the Gillandite line,* Sam remembered, as he guided his knights to the Rook Division of the Clawlandite army. Arrows and javelins rained down on them from the giant elephants, and one of Sam's best knights fell. Sam knew how to fight off elephants easily, though. He ordered his riders to charge at the elephants at full speed and plunge their swords into the creatures' soft feet. Sure enough, the elephants were scared and ran off the battle field.

Sam looked around to see if he could spot Honey, but could see him nowhere. There was no time to think about Honey, as the Bishop Division of the Clawlandite army was moving to attack them, just as planned. They were not so easy to defeat as they rode in chariots and were far more heavily armed, including heavy spears that could easily penetrate a knight's light armour. Three more of Sam's knights fell before the already weakened Bishop Division was defeated. Only Sam and a newly qualified knight remained.

Meanwhile, Honey seemed to be having the time of his life. The other Rooks had given him the job of steering the elephant and he enjoyed it immensely, for he didn't have to do any fighting. All Honey had to do was try and stop the elephant from stepping on the opposing soldiers, which he had been told was the wrong thing to do. He didn't like the idea of being stepped on by such a massive creature himself, and didn't think the Clawlandites would like it any better; he seemed to forget that he was in a battle! He began to talk to the elephant, which swished its huge ears backward and forwards in response. It sometimes even lifted its trunk and gave a long trumpeting cry. Honey became fond of his new elephant friend and decided it was the best thing in the world to be in the Rook Division of the army.

On the other side of the battlefield, Sam moved to combat a small division of normal soldiers. It wasn't too hard to defeat them, but his last knight was approached from behind by one of the soldiers and killed. He began to realise the horrors of this battle, as he remembered how young his last knight was, how he had watched him being knighted just two years ago.

Now Sam was on his own. His next move was a free one and he had time to stop for a short while. He looked around and saw, to his dismay, the Gillandite army diminished to a few divisions and he saw friends he had known for years fighting and being killed and lying dead or wounded. The Gillandite army would not last until nightfall.

But Sam had to leave the battle now. He had to leave the story of Gilland and he had to conclude his own little life. His next move was to duel with Lord Mould and meet his death. This was how his father, Rocky, had met his death, and Sam was not afraid to walk in his footsteps.

The roar of the battle seemed to fade in his ears as he approached the menacing figure of Lord Mould. The Clawlandite King was more fearful than Sam could ever have expected. His form was unrecognisable, as he was deformed by rankling mould and slime. His eyes had the same fire of the burning of Gilland in them, and the rest of his face was covered by a hood of mould.

Lord Mould brandished his sword, dripping with mould and slime. By his side stood the creature that was his pet, its teeth seeming yellower and its eyes redder as it stood grinning at Sam. Sam dismounted his horse and walked slowly to Lord Mould. He lifted his golden sword and it caught the gleam of the sun streaming through a break in the clouds.

Chapter 19

The Last Piece of the Puzzle

Sam brought his sword down heavily, but Lord Mould's met it with a tremendous force that sent a pain along Sam's arms. Again Sam bore his sword down, and again Lord Mould's heavier sword met it. Lord Mould's pet grinned more and more as every blow of Sam's sword fell useless. All his skill now seemed like a squire's compared to Lord Mould.

He stopped his useless blows and Lord Mould started attacking Sam with much more vigour than Sam had ever met before. He was hard put to ward off the blows. Someone tossed him a shield but the first blow to it from Lord Mould's sword smashed it in pieces. Sam began to pant from exhaustion after the first five minutes, but he would not give in.

The duel went on and on, and neither sword touched either Sam or Lord Mould, but Sam's strength was slowly giving way. Eventually, one mighty blow to Sam's sword found Sam panting on the ground. Every muscle in his body seemed to ache and he was so weak he could hardly hold up his head. Sam could see that the battle was almost lost but could do no more than wait for the final blow from Lord Mould. The sun began to sink below the mountains and covered everything with a blood red tint.

Lord Mould raised his sword to kill Sam. He brought it down but it crashed against someone else's sword before it reached Sam. Sam looked up to see Honey bearing down on Lord Mould. Lord Mould turned his attention to Honey and they were soon locked in a vicious duel.

'No one's going to hurt my little brother!' said Honey. Sam had never seen Honey so powerful-looking and so magnificent.

Lord Mould seemed to struggle to keep off the blows. But the fire in Lord Mould's eyes seemed to leap up as he brought his sword down on Honey's right arm. Honey cried out with pain from the wound, but quickly took his sword in his left paw to carry on the duel.

Honey's eyes flashed with anger and the red part of his eye glowed like a fire. One blow from Honey's sword and Lord Mould's sword flew out of his hands. Lord Mould was at the mercy of Honey now and Honey knew what he must do, but his eyes softened and his paw quivered and he held his sword still. Sam could not understand Honey's hesitation; this was the chance to save Gilland.

'I can't kill you,' Honey said to Lord Mould. 'Firstly because only your bloodline can kill you; and secondly, I can't feel anger towards you, just pity.'

'Kill me, Honey,' Lord Mould's voice sounded more distant and more like a lost memory than ever. 'Kill me and become the King I should have been.'

'I'm sorry,' Honey closed his eyes and brought down his sword on Lord Mould. The battle seemed to pause as everyone stared in astonishment at Lord Mould lying dead on the ground. The second-in-command of the Clawlandite army took over, and Sam was horrified to see the battle continue.

The Gillandite army was now very small and almost wiped out. He watched as Gilland was slowly being defeated, despite what had just happened. Killing Lord Mould was not the key to immediate victory as Sam had supposed. But his mind turned to Honey. Honey's arm was badly wounded and needed attention immediately, but Honey was staring at something else.

Lord Mould's pet had not been killed, but as soon as Lord Mould died it began to act very oddly. It kept rolling on the ground and scraping itself against anything metallic it could find. Its form had also changed and it looked small and cat-like. It kept rubbing and scraping until it began to scrape the mould and slime off itself. A fur coat, underneath the mould, began to appear. It was a tawny colour with black spots. Sam watched the creature as it made one final roll on the ground to clean its coat. And then, stood before them, was a young leopard cub.

'Tenga!' cried Sam.

Just then the sky was filled with a vast cloud of birds of all kinds, and an army of rabbits covered the ground, both headed by the Great Eagle. They swooped down on the Clawlandite army and soon the enemy warriors were fleeing for their lives.

'Victory! Victory!' King Farratol cried as the remnant of the Gillandite army crowded to him. Sam managed to get onto his horse with Tenga and Honey and ride to the doctor. He left Honey there, and took Tenga to the King. He met the King in one of the Clawlandite tents talking to the Great Eagle. Sam showed Tenga to King Farratol.

'Apparently,' said the King to Sam, 'the Great Eagle knew that Lord Mould had turned Tenga into his pet and was all ready and waiting in case Lord Mould was killed and the curse lifted from Tenga.'

'All those travels,' said Sam smiling, 'and we had actually met Tenga along the way a number of times, trying to stop us from finding him.'

'My thoughts were not my own then,' said Tenga, and he began to relate what had happened to him.

He was taken by the Gronad to his cave and had an exciting time there; but then the Gronad took him to a lonely castle in Clawland and Lord Mould corrupted him. He didn't remember much of when he was Lord Mould's pet, all he remembered was pain and shadow.

'I was told by the Gronad that you told him to bring Tenga to Lord Mould,' said Sam to the Great Eagle, 'saying it was a gift.'

'I wanted Gilland to fight the beginning of the battle on their own,' replied the Great Eagle. 'I knew that Lord Mould's son would kill Lord Mould, and I wanted that to happen, because I began to realise that Lord Mould's son would not turn out like the evil King of Clawland, but instead showed true qualities. I wanted him to show a disloyalty to Lord Mould and show the quality of love to his adopted brother before I would recognise him as King of Clawland.'

Sam did not quite believe that the Great Eagle had unselfish motives in this all. No, the Eagle was a far too proud and cunning fellow. But Sam decided to keep these thoughts to himself.

Then he asked, 'Who's Lord Mould's son?'

'Honey is Lord Mould's son.'

Sam felt queer. 'So he's not my brother?'

'No. When Honey was a tiny puppy his mother died and Lord Mould looked after him. This was before Lord Mould was corrupted. He loved his son. But by the time Honey was three years old, Lord Mould changed towards him because Honey showed a great lack of intelligence and Lord Mould did not want him to have the throne, so he cast him out into the freezing cold to die. I found him there and was going to kill him because he was the son of my mortal enemy. But just as I began to swoop down on the tiny pup, Rocky, your father, was riding along and managed to snatch up Honey before I could kill him.'

That was what that tapestry was all about! thought Sam.

'After Lord Mould cast Honey out, he was struck with a feeling of guilt that he could not control,' the Great Eagle continued, after stretching his wings. 'He searched for months and months to find Honey, but your father kept him secret and told everyone that he was your older brother. Lord Mould eventually gave up the search and put all Honey's toys and cot in the top of a tower, hoping for his return one day. His guilt grew so immense that he decided to drown it in making war and greedily taking anything he could lay his hands on. He became cruel and hardened and thus corrupted himself until he turned into that mouldy creature.'

'So Lord Mould was a dog?' Sam could hardly believe the tale he was hearing.

'Indeed, the gentlest dog you could find.' The Great Eagle scratched at the table to sharpen his claws, then continued with Honey's story. 'Years later, I found Honey on the beach at the other end of the world, and tried to kill him. I was sure that he would turn out like Lord Mould if he took the throne, and I knew his past was bound to be discovered. But just as I was about to kill him, Lord Mould came galloping up on his dark horse and attacked me and saved his son. And you know the rest.'

'How did you know Honey was Lord Mould's missing son?' Sam still could not believe the story.

'One half of his left eye is red. Although your father said that it turned that way from an accident, it is really inherited from Lord Mould.'

Sam was suddenly struck with a realisation. 'This means that Honey is now King of Clawland!'

'Yes, indeed. I will perform the coronation ceremony myself as soon as all is cleared and Honey is better.' The Great Eagle hopped outside the tent. 'I must go now.' He stretched his wings and flew off to his castle, followed by the other birds and rabbits.

Sam went immediately to the doctor's tent to find Honey. To his dismay he saw Honey with only one arm – his right arm had been amputated.

'How are you doing, Honey-buns?' Sam tried to sound as cheerful as possible.

'Oh fine. I've already thought up a song about

the battle.'

Sam smiled. Although Honey was not really his brother, they would stay brothers at heart.

'You know Sammy, I don't think I can stay in Gilland, my heart is with the Endworlders. They really appreciate my talent.'

Sam then told him that he was now to be the King of Clawland. Honey was delighted.

'I'd love that,' said Honey, wagging his tail. 'I liked the castle there; it seemed familiar somehow and I seemed to half remember happy times connected with it.'

Sam decided not to tell Honey that he was Lord Mould's son, because he probably wouldn't have understood. Indeed, Sam could hardly understand it himself!

Suddenly it seemed that the last piece of a puzzle had been found, and he began to realise that everything fitted together perfectly. Mystery had taken off her veil and revealed long-kept secrets.

Chapter 20

After the Battle

Before we leave Sam and Honey and their friends, a few words must be said about their lives after the battle.

Soon after Gilland's victory, Honey and Sam and a few others went to Clawland for Honey's coronation. The Great Eagle performed the ceremony as promised, and Honey sat quite patiently on the throne while the Great Eagle placed the crown on his head.

'Hail Honey, King of Clawland!' the Great Eagle cried, and the Clawlandites echoed his words throughout the throne room and the city.

Immediately after this part of the ceremony was completed, Honey stood up on the throne and cleared his voice.

'Thanks everyone for letting me be your King, it was very nice of you. I rather like Clawland, and I've made a special song to celebrate this special day.'

Sam rolled his eyes and smiled at Truss.

Honey got out a very inky piece of paper and started to sing.

'I am King today,
Hip, hip hooray!
Now I can sing all day;
"Honey's so clever" you'll say!'

The Clawlandites looked doubtfully at each other. But at least their new king was better than Lord Mould, they thought. Indeed, Clawland prospered greatly under Honey's rule. The theatres, banqueting halls and colleges were reopened and houses and buildings repaired. Overall, the city began to look a brighter place.

After a few months of living in Clawland, Honey's thoughts turned to the Endworlder village. He eventually left the throne to Truss to look after as steward and went to live with the Endworlders. He was very happy there and learned to use his left paw for everything, including writing poems and drawing pictures. The Endworlders regarded him as a hero, and indeed he was. He even went to visit the Gronad every other day, and would always bring a jewel or a piece of gold for his collection.

As for Sam, he refused an offer from Honey to become the commander of the Clawlandite army, saying that his loyalties lay with Gilland. After that, he married Maddy. And Honey did not forget about singing the song at their wedding, but Sam didn't mind anymore, and Maddy was delighted. Sam and Maddy then settled down in Sam and Honey's childhood home and adopted Tenga.

Sam watched with delight as Tenga grew up and become a mighty knight like he had been. A number of years of this happiness were to last and then, when King Farratol died at a ripe old age, probably from playing chess too much, the throne would be left to Tenga.

And from his high castle, the Great Eagle brooded, watching greedily as the lands of Clawland and Gilland grew strong and wealthy.

THE END

ISBN 142515867-6

9 781425 158675